BOOK 4: Fur Ball of the Apocalypse

…h grader Derrick's goldfish, Finn and Gillian, have gone missing—but so have Derrick's two science teachers. Max and Derrick are on the case... but they could be headed for a fur ball of a dead end!

About the series

Middle school can be survival of the "fitting-in" at best.In *Dead Max Comix*, Derrick discovers that his secrets aren't really unusual. A light-hearted touch at accepting yourself and finding your own "pack".

BOOK 3
DEAD MAX COMIX
By Dana Sullivan
BULLY FOR YOU!

Book 1: The Deadening
Released January 2020
HC: 978-1-63440-852-3
PB: 978-1-63440-853-0

BOOK 4
DEAD MAX COMIX
By Dana Sullivan
FURBALL OF THE APOCALYPSE!

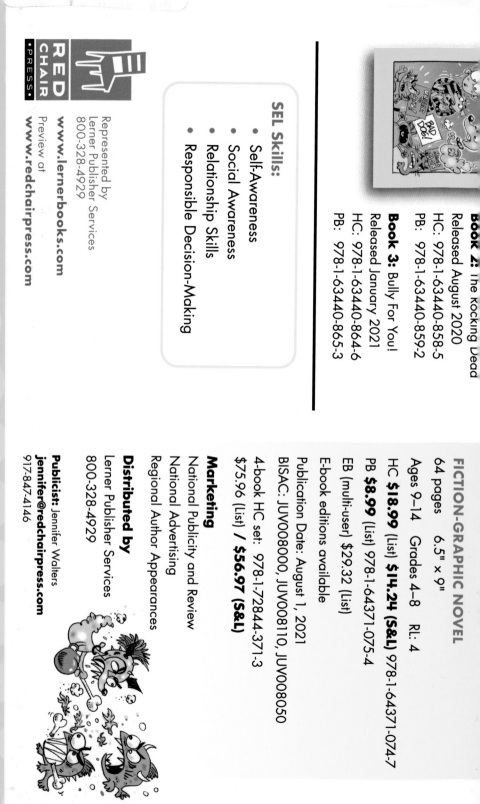

FICTION-GRAPHIC NOVEL

64 pages   6.5" x 9"

Ages 9–14   Grades 4–8   RL: 4

HC **$18.99** (List) **$14.24 (S&L)** 978-1-64371-074-7

PB **$8.99** (List) 978-1-64371-075-4

EB (multi-user) $29.32 (List)

E-book editions available

Publication Date: August 1, 2021

BISAC: JUV008000, JUV008110, JUV008050

4-book HC set: 978-1-72844-371-3

$75.96 (List) / **$56.97 (S&L)**

Marketing

National Publicity and Review

National Advertising

Regional Author Appearances

Distributed by

Lerner Publisher Services

800-328-4929

Publicist: Jennifer Walters

jennifer@redchairpress.com

917-847-4146

Book 2: The Rocking Dead

Released August 2020

HC: 978-1-63440-858-5

PB: 978-1-63440-859-2

Book 3: Bully For You!

Released January 2021

HC: 978-1-63440-864-6

PB: 978-1-63440-865-3

SEL Skills:

- Self-Awareness
- Social Awareness
- Relationship Skills
- Responsible Decision-Making

RED CHAIR ·PRESS·

Represented by
Lerner Publisher Services
800-328-4929

www.lernerbooks.com

Preview at
www.redchairpress.com

DEAD MAX COMIX

FURBALL OF THE APOCALYPSE!

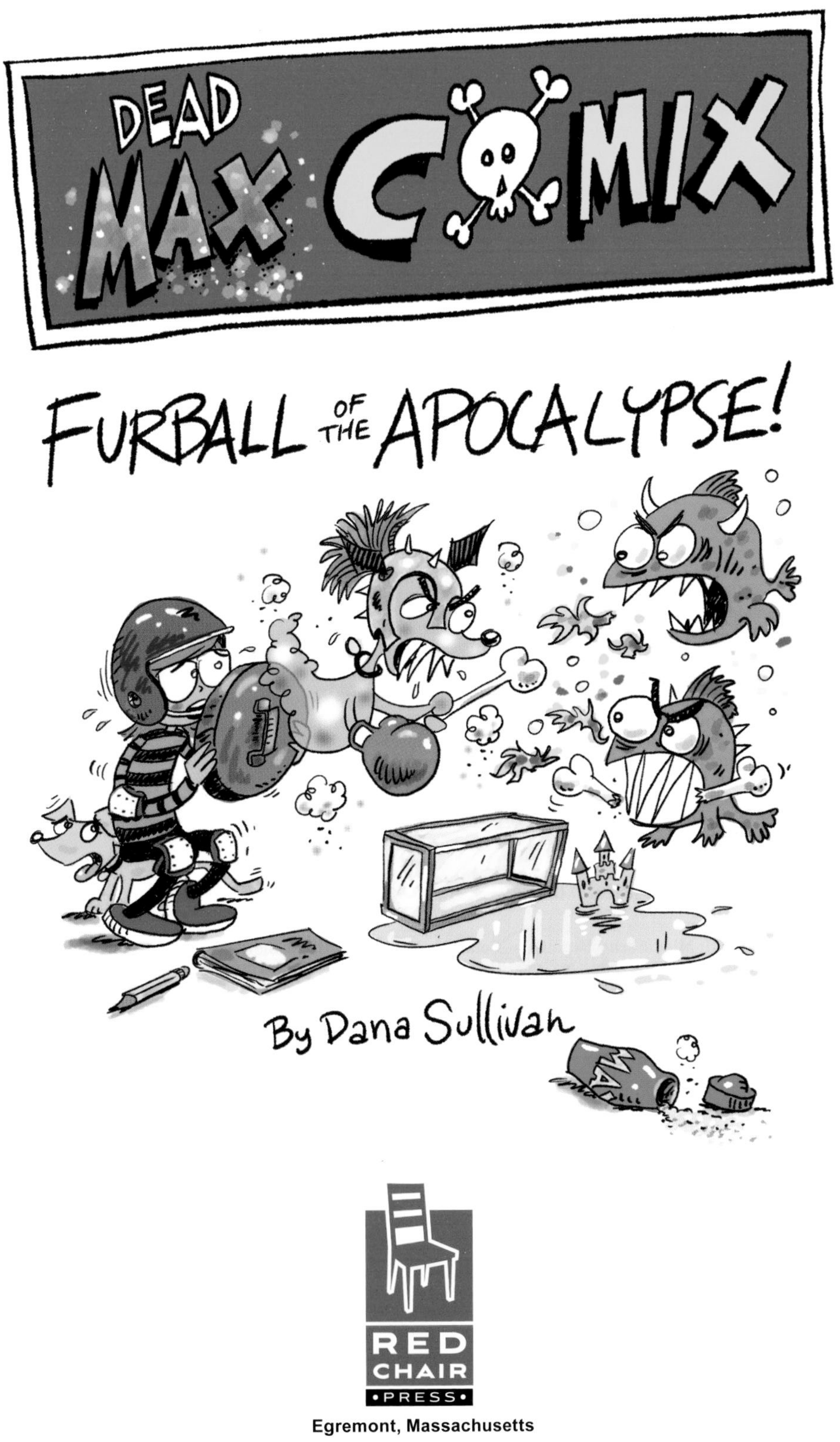

By Dana Sullivan

RED CHAIR PRESS

Egremont, Massachusetts

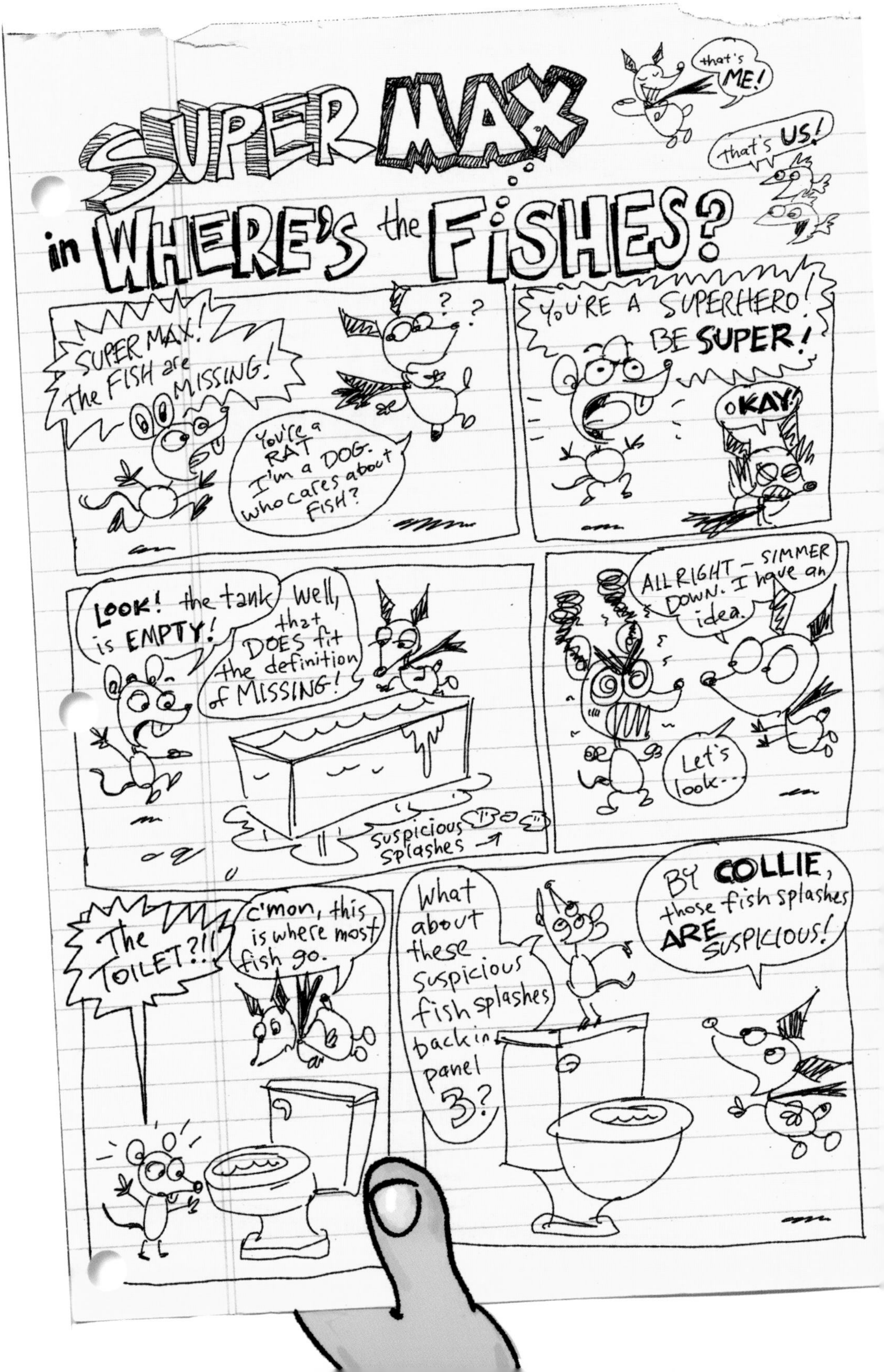
SUPER MAX
that's ME!
that's US!
in WHERE'S the FISHES?
SUPER MAX! the FISH are MISSING!
You're a RAT. I'm a DOG. Who cares about FISH?
YOU'RE A SUPERHERO! BE SUPER!
OKAY!
LOOK! the tank is EMPTY!
Well, that DOES fit the definition of MISSING!
suspicious splashes
ALL RIGHT – SIMMER DOWN. I have an idea.
Let's look...
The TOILET?!!
C'mon, this is where most fish go.
What about these suspicious fish splashes back in panel 3?
BY COLLIE, those fish splashes ARE SUSPICIOUS!

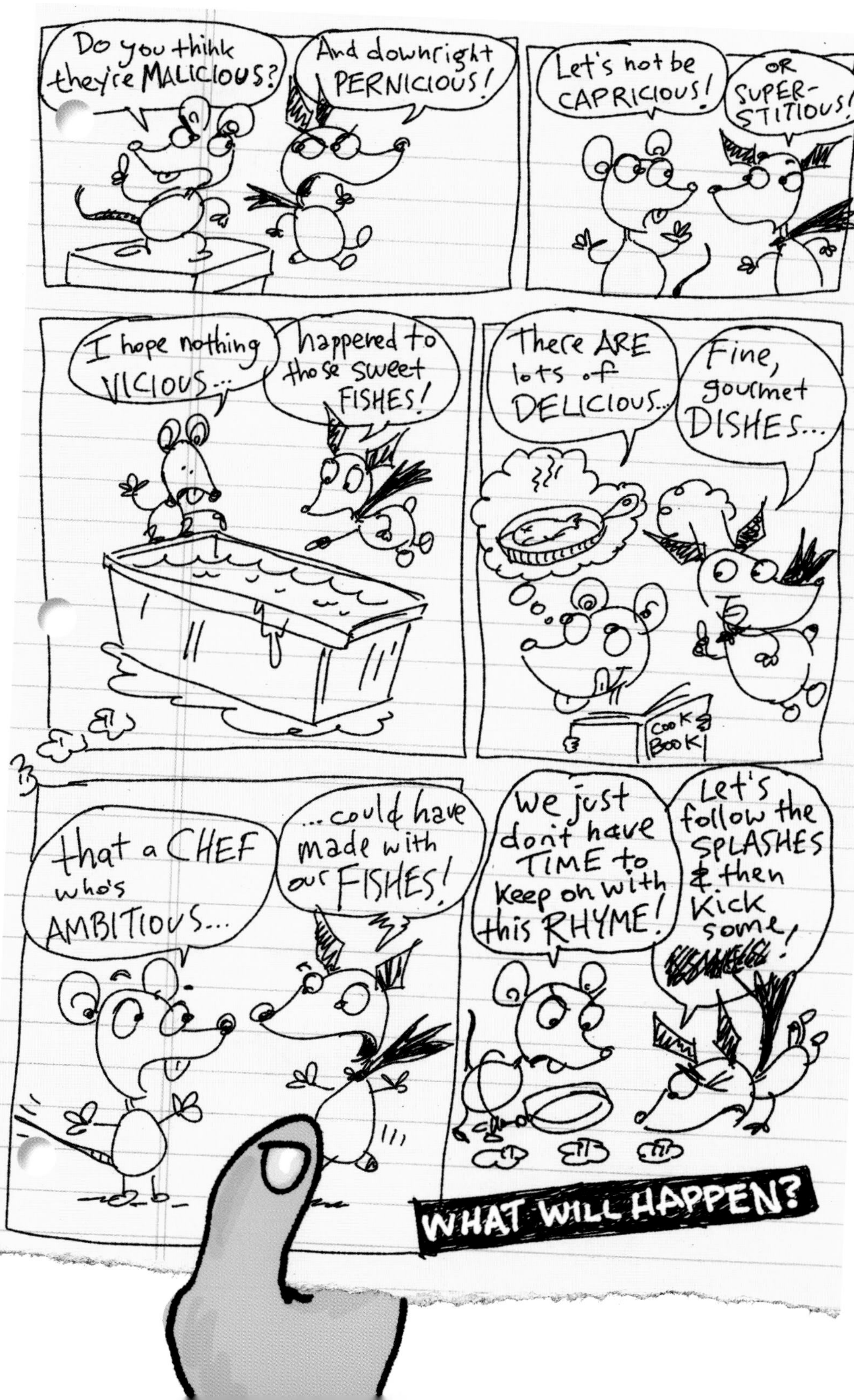

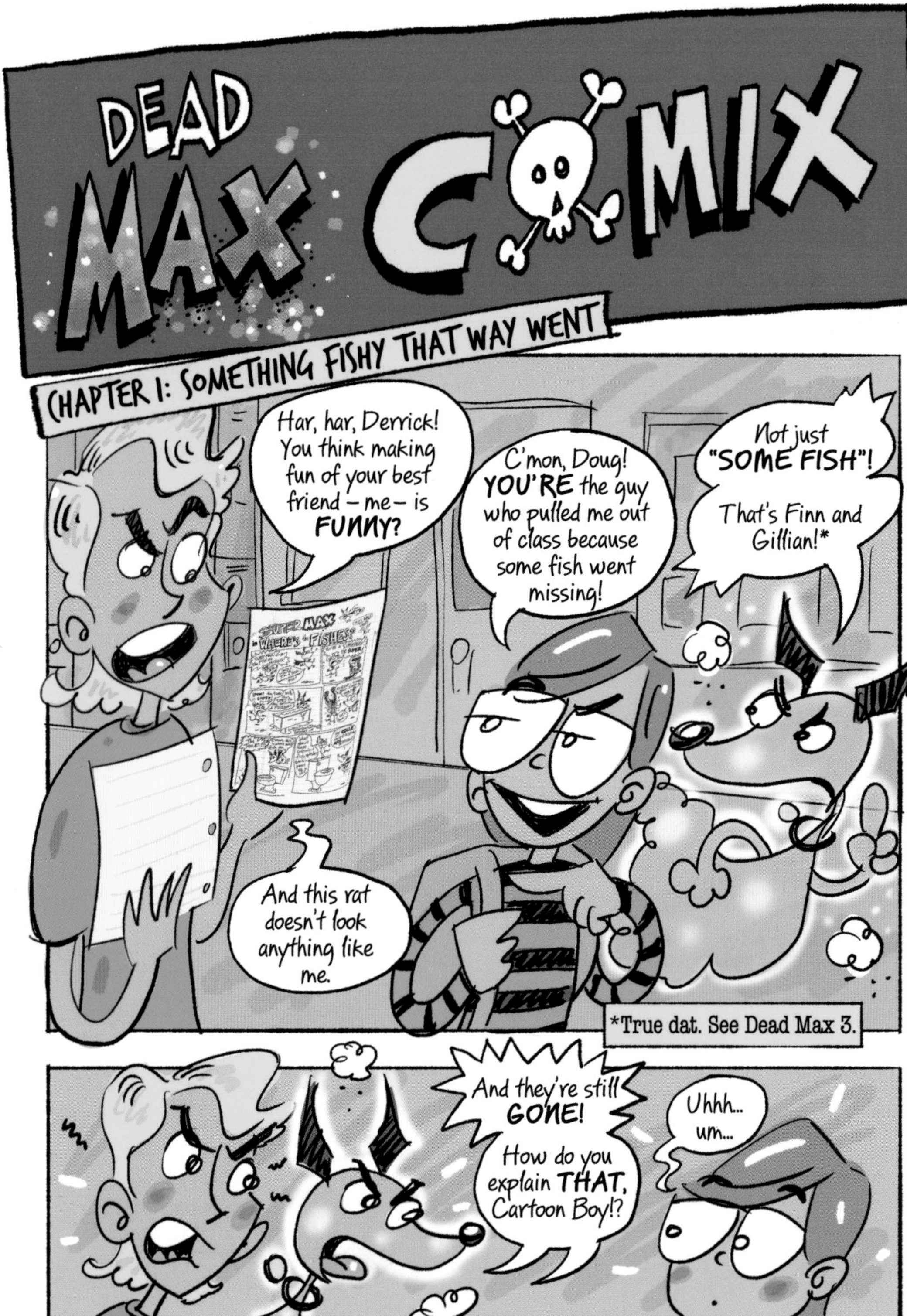
DEAD MAX COMIX
CHAPTER 1: SOMETHING FISHY THAT WAY WENT
Har, har, Derrick! You think making fun of your best friend – me – is FUNNY?
C'mon, Doug! YOU'RE the guy who pulled me out of class because some fish went missing!
Not just "SOME FISH"! That's Finn and Gillian!*
SUPER MAX in WHERE'S the FISHES?
And this rat doesn't look anything like me.
*True dat. See Dead Max 3.
And they're still GONE!
How do you explain THAT, Cartoon Boy!?
Uhhh... um...

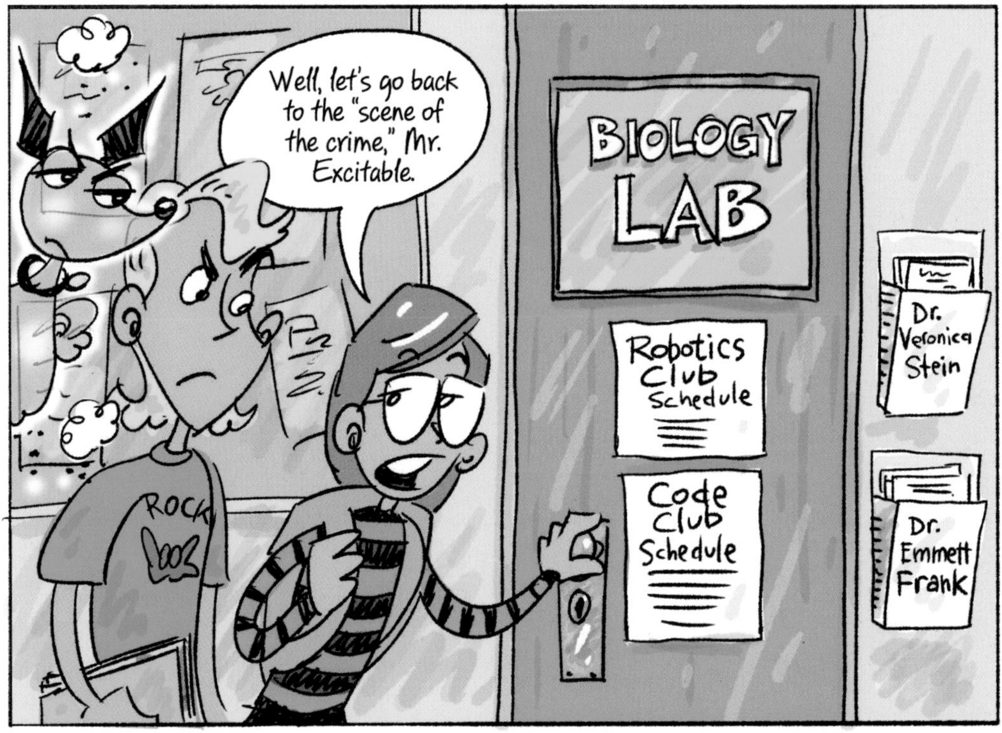

Well, let's go back to the "scene of the crime," Mr. Excitable.
BIOLOGY LAB
Robotics Club Schedule
Code Club Schedule
Dr. Veronica Stein
Dr. Emmett Frank
ROCK

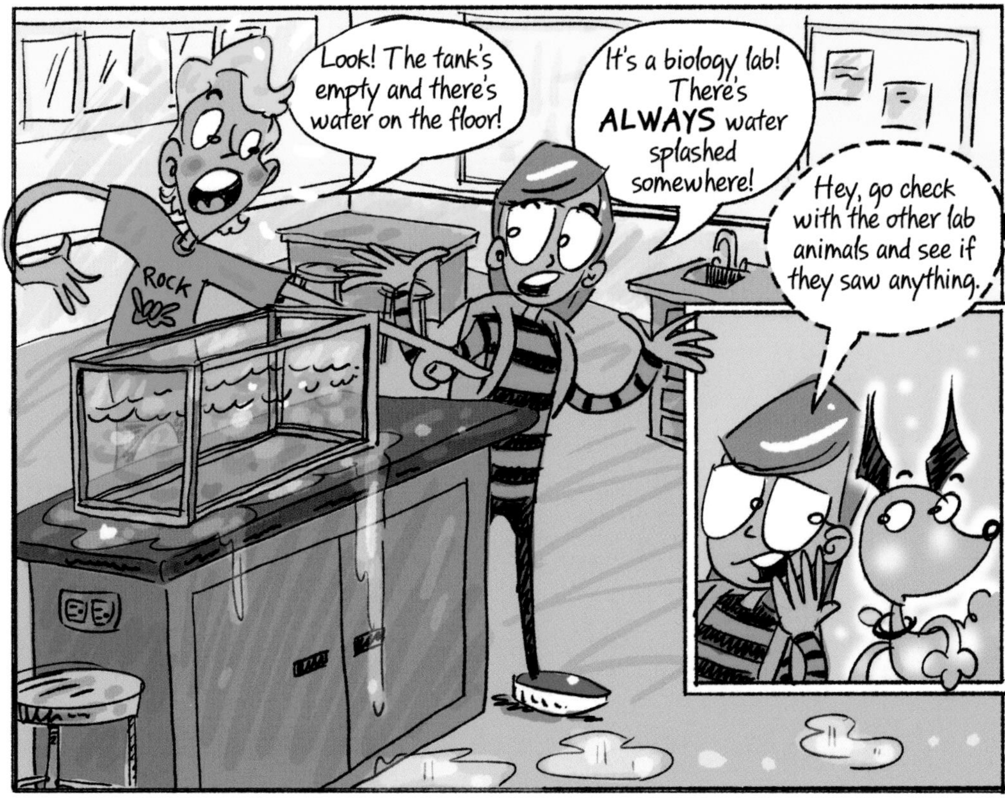

Look! The tank's empty and there's water on the floor!
It's a biology lab! There's **ALWAYS** water splashed somewhere!
Hey, go check with the other lab animals and see if they saw anything.
ROCK

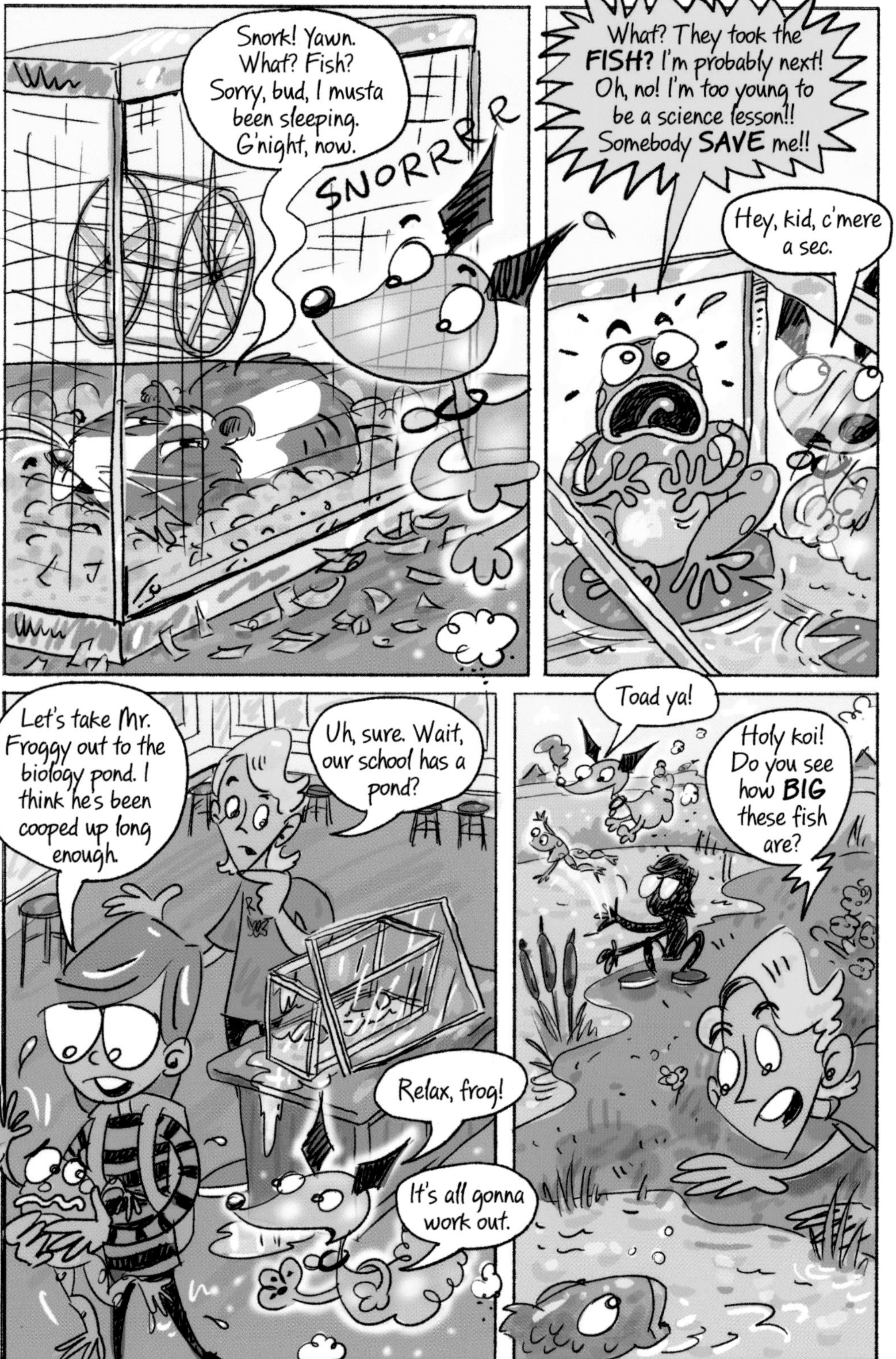
Snork! Yawn. What? Fish? Sorry, bud, I musta been sleeping. G'night, now.
SNORRRR
What? They took the **FISH?** I'm probably next! Oh, no! I'm too young to be a science lesson!! Somebody **SAVE** me!!
Hey, kid, c'mere a sec.
Let's take Mr. Froggy out to the biology pond. I think he's been cooped up long enough.
Uh, sure. Wait, our school has a pond?
Relax, frog!
It's all gonna work out.
Toad ya!
Holy koi! Do you see how **BIG** these fish are?

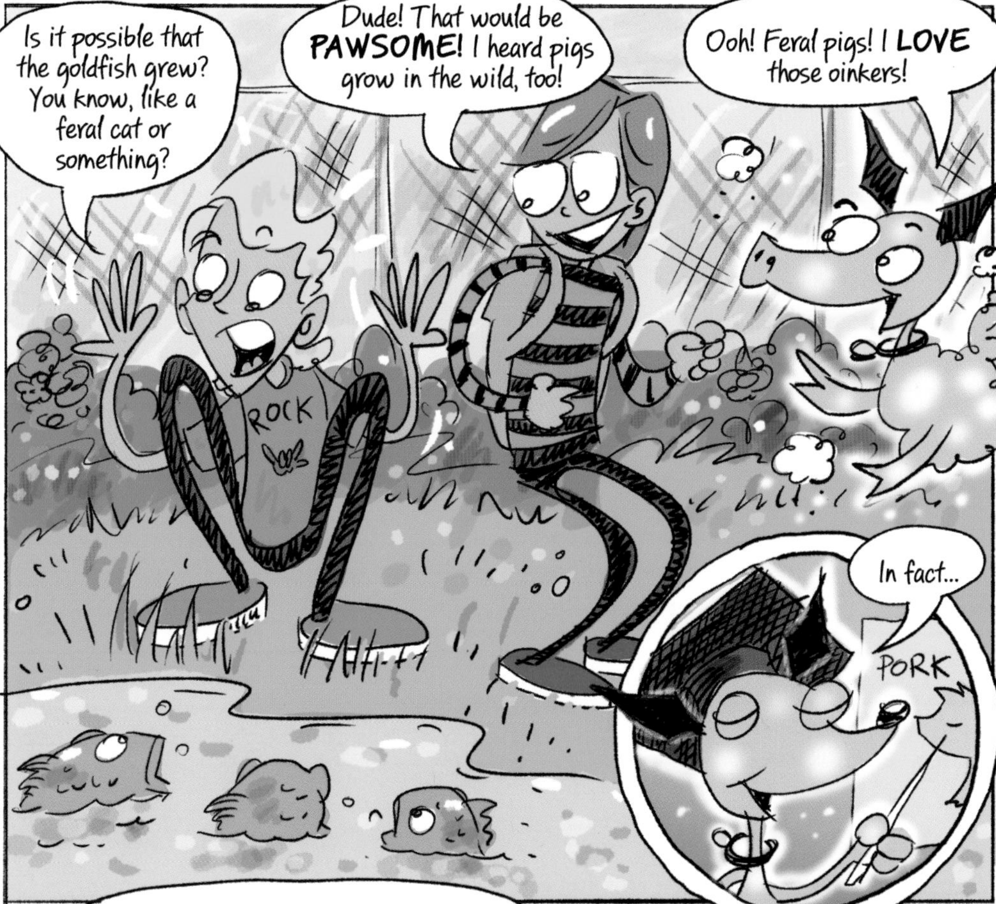
Is it possible that the goldfish grew? You know, like a feral cat or something?
Dude! That would be **PAWSOME!** I heard pigs grow in the wild, too!
Ooh! Feral pigs! I **LOVE** those oinkers!
ROCK
In fact...
PORK

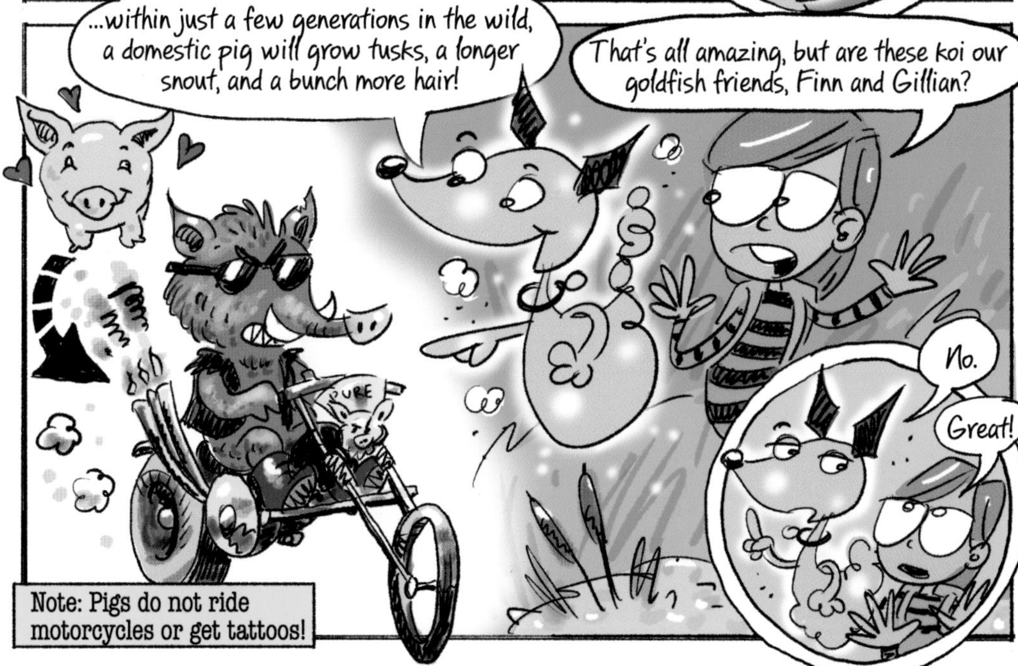
...within just a few generations in the wild, a domestic pig will grow tusks, a longer snout, and a bunch more hair!
That's all amazing, but are these koi our goldfish friends, Finn and Gillian?
PURE
No.
Great!
Note: Pigs do not ride motorcycles or get tattoos!

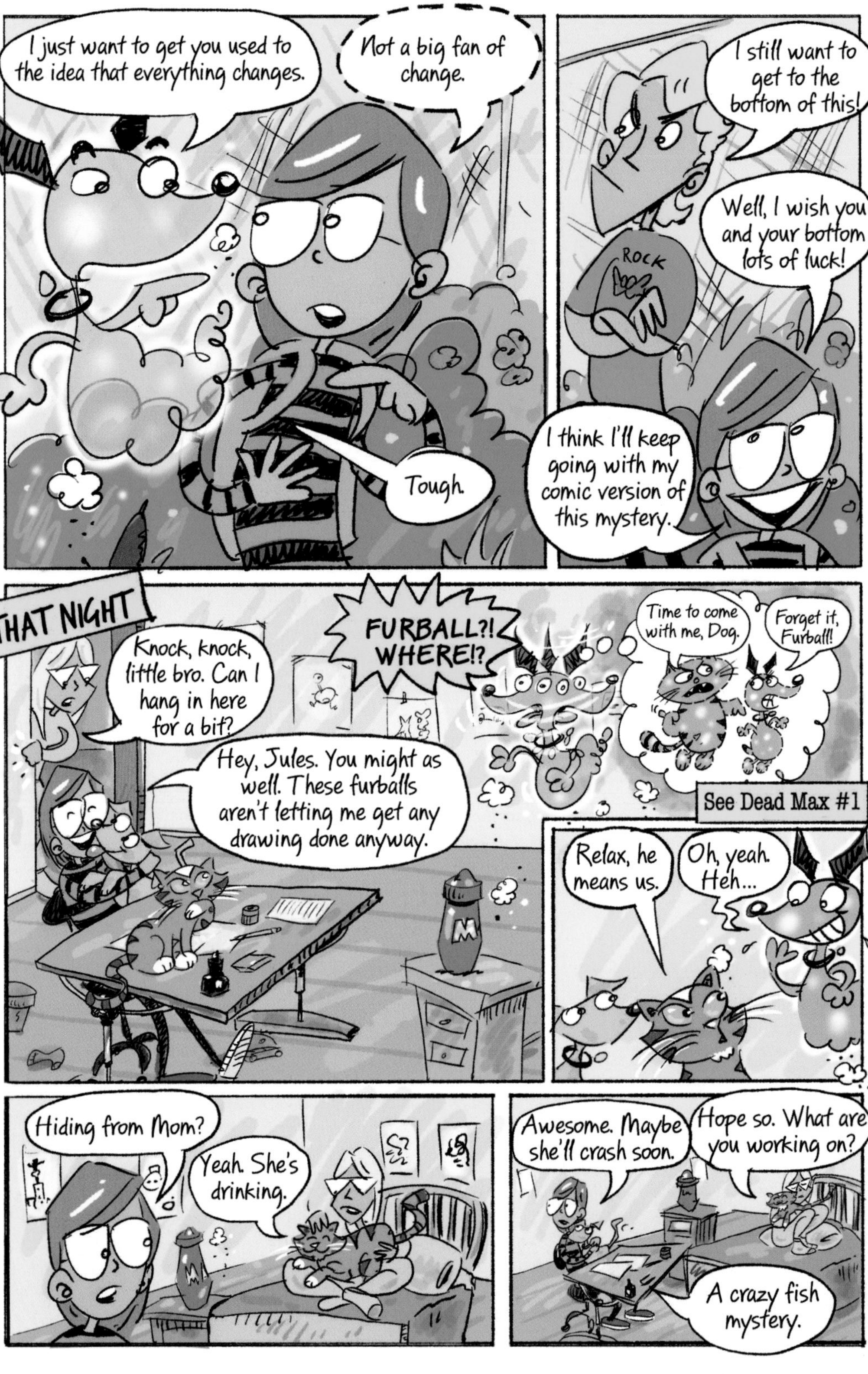

I just want to get you used to the idea that everything changes.
Not a big fan of change.
Tough.
I still want to get to the bottom of this!
ROCK
Well, I wish you and your bottom lots of luck!
I think I'll keep going with my comic version of this mystery.
THAT NIGHT
Knock, knock, little bro. Can I hang in here for a bit?
Hey, Jules. You might as well. These furballs aren't letting me get any drawing done anyway.
FURBALL?! WHERE!?
Time to come with me, Dog.
Forget it, Furball!
See Dead Max #1
Relax, he means us.
Oh, yeah. Heh...
Hiding from Mom?
Yeah. She's drinking.
Awesome. Maybe she'll crash soon.
Hope so. What are you working on?
A crazy fish mystery.

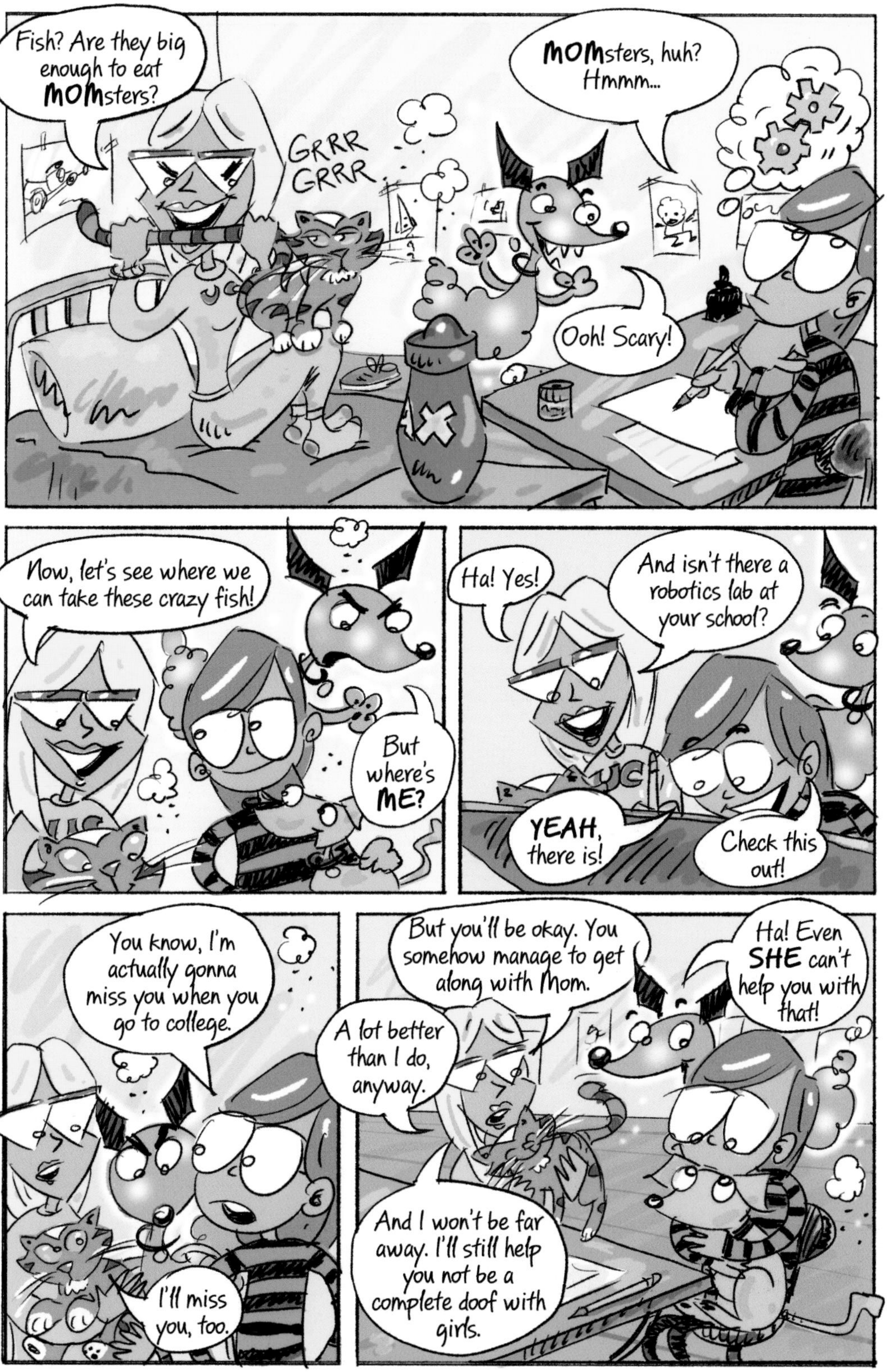
Fish? Are they big enough to eat MOMsters?
GRRR GRRR
MOMsters, huh? Hmmm...
Ooh! Scary!
Now, let's see where we can take these crazy fish!
But where's ME?
Ha! Yes!
And isn't there a robotics lab at your school?
YEAH, there is!
Check this out!
You know, I'm actually gonna miss you when you go to college.
I'll miss you, too.
But you'll be okay. You somehow manage to get along with Mom.
A lot better than I do, anyway.
Ha! Even SHE can't help you with that!
And I won't be far away. I'll still help you not be a complete doof with girls.

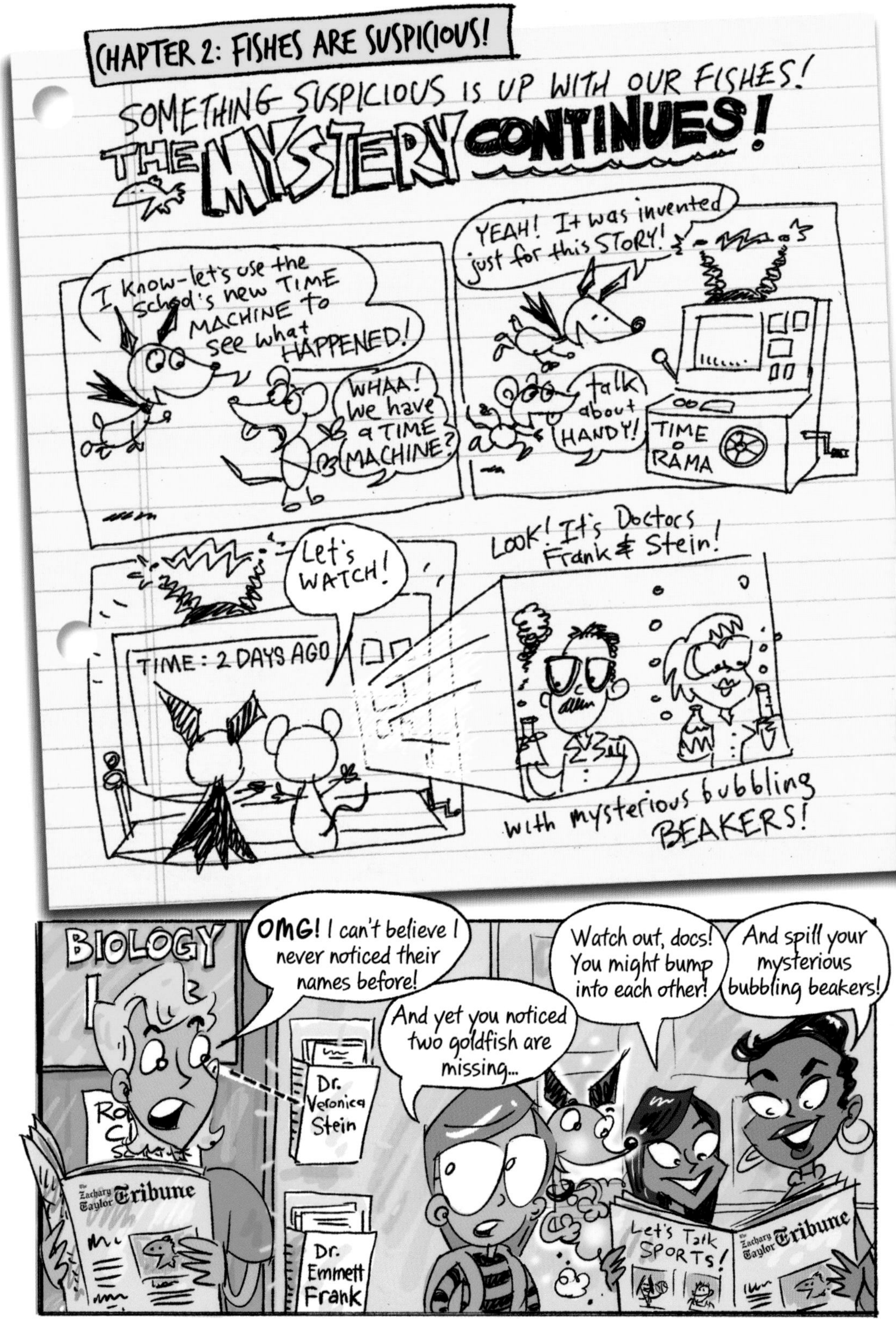
CHAPTER 2: FISHES ARE SUSPICIOUS!
SOMETHING SUSPICIOUS IS UP WITH OUR FISHES!
THE MYSTERY CONTINUES!
I know-let's use the school's new TIME MACHINE to see what HAPPENED!
WHAA! We have a TIME MACHINE?
YEAH! It was invented just for this STORY!
talk about HANDY!
TIME O RAMA
Let's WATCH!
TIME: 2 DAYS AGO
LOOK! It's Doctors Frank & Stein!
with mysterious bubbling BEAKERS!
BIOLOGY
OMG! I can't believe I never noticed their names before!
And yet you noticed two goldfish are missing...
Watch out, docs! You might bump into each other!
And spill your mysterious bubbling beakers!
Dr. Veronica Stein
Dr. Emmett Frank
The Zachary Taylor Tribune
Let's Talk SPORTS!
The Zachary Taylor Tribune

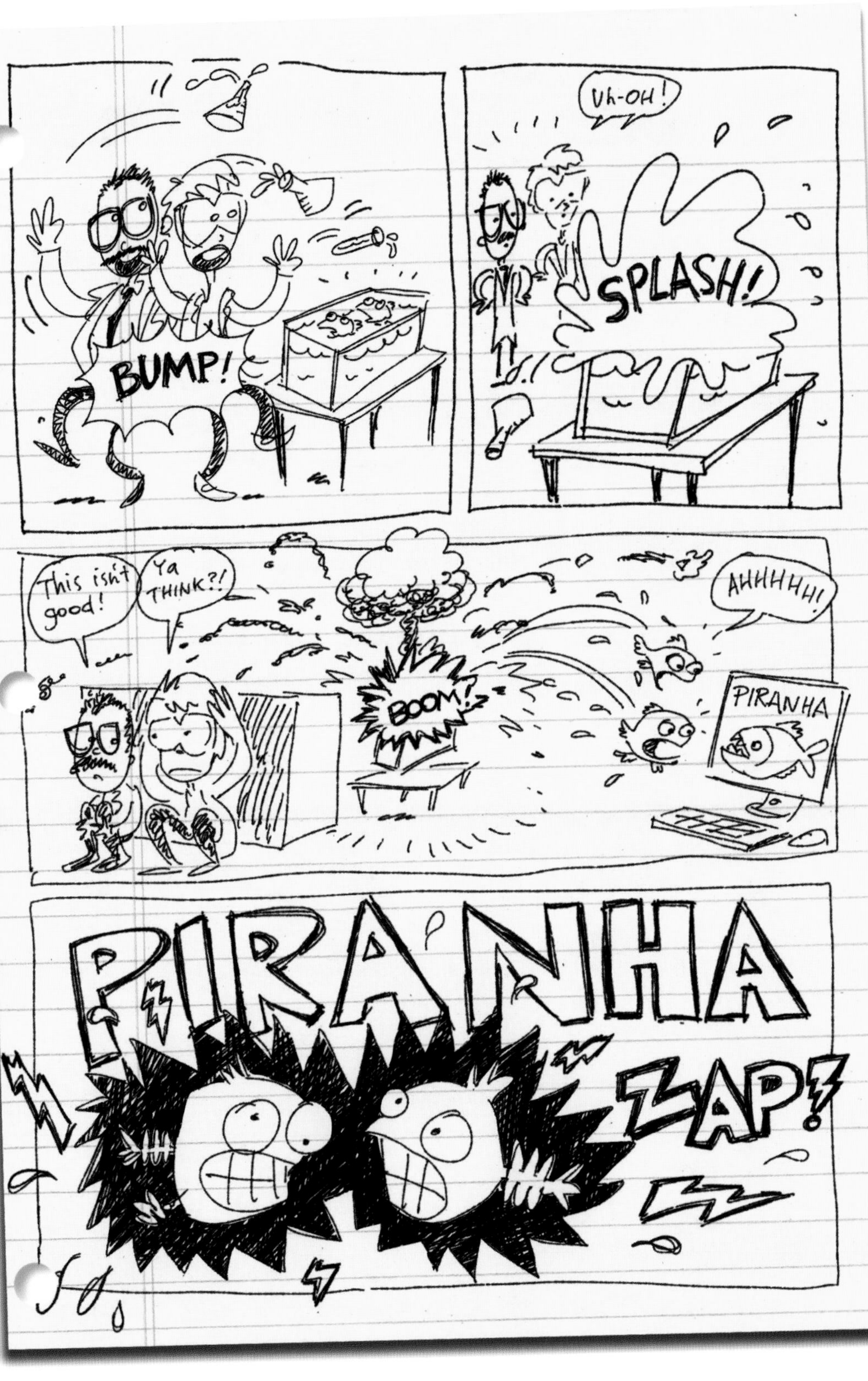
BUMP!
Uh-OH!
SPLASH!
This isn't good!
Ya THINK?!
BOOM!
AHHHHH!
PIRANHA
PIRANHA
ZAP!

GASP!
Hey Finn, you look like a PIRANHA!
GASP!
You DO TOO, GILLIAN!
GASP!
PUFF
FLOP!
FLOP!
PUFF
PUFF
PUFF
PUFF!
FLOP
I guess even PIRANHAS can't breathe out of WATER!
GASP
we must have TRANSMOGRIFIED when our wet selves hit the keyboard!
Let's roll off this table into that convenient pail of WATER!
ROLL
ROLL
Great idea! I hope they're not too cheesed off that we destroyed their computer!
SAFETY NOTICE
In case of excessive DRYNESS, use water in pail
OXY
ACET
PAIL OF WATER
DANGER
TURN SIDE-WAYS
WAAAA!
PAIL OF WATER

OOF!
I think we missed...
Looks like we landed on a pile of ZOMBIE Comics!
ZOMBIE TALES
ZOMBIE TALES
Note: Yes, they can read. They're in a school!
Keep ROLLING! We gotta make it to that water!
Oy vey!
oh NO! The Zombie comics are rolling up around us.
The curse of being wet little fishies!
CRASH!
WOBBLE
KLONK
WOBBLE!
I made it!
OXY
ACETYL
DANGE
PAIL OF WATER
I feel water! I think we're OKAY!
PSHHH!
PSHHH!
ACETY
DAN
CAUTION!
PAIL WAT
ZOMBI TAL
ZOMBI TAL

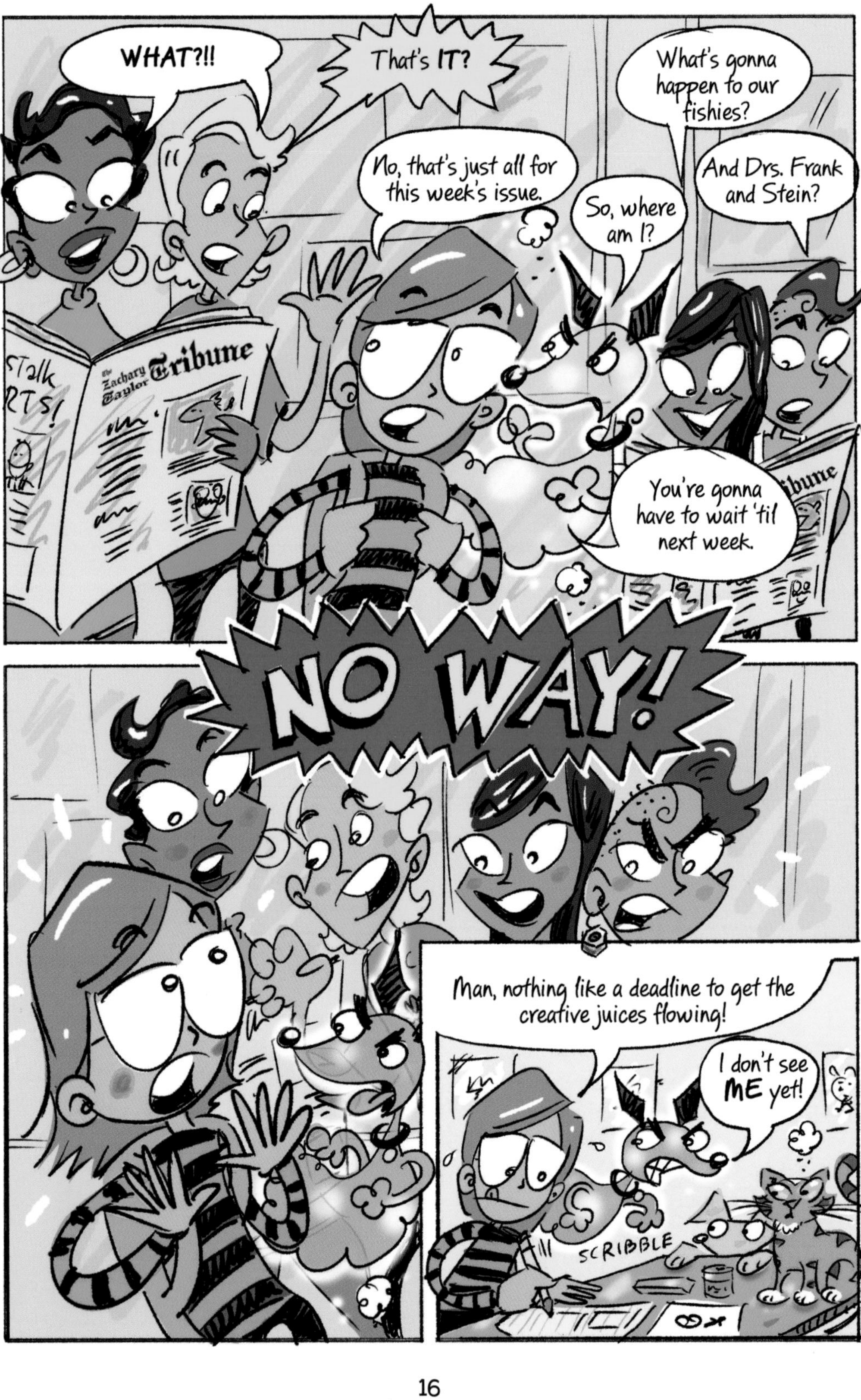
WHAT?!!
That's IT?
The Zachary Taylor Tribune
No, that's just all for this week's issue.
What's gonna happen to our fishies?
So, where am I?
And Drs. Frank and Stein?
You're gonna have to wait 'til next week.
NO WAY!
Man, nothing like a deadline to get the creative juices flowing!
I don't see ME yet!
SCRIBBLE

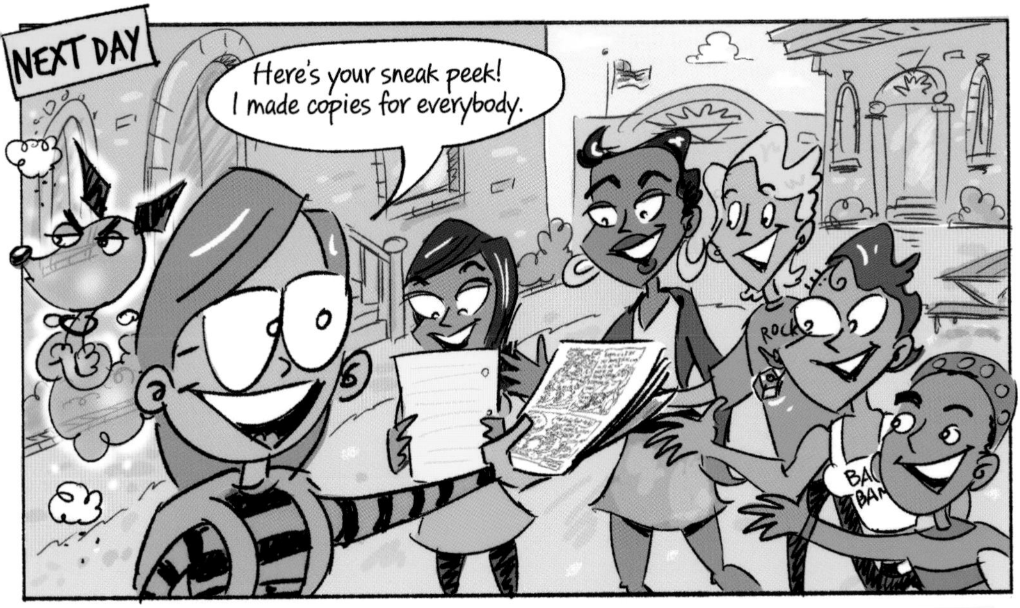
NEXT DAY
Here's your sneak peek! I made copies for everybody.
ROCK
BA BAN

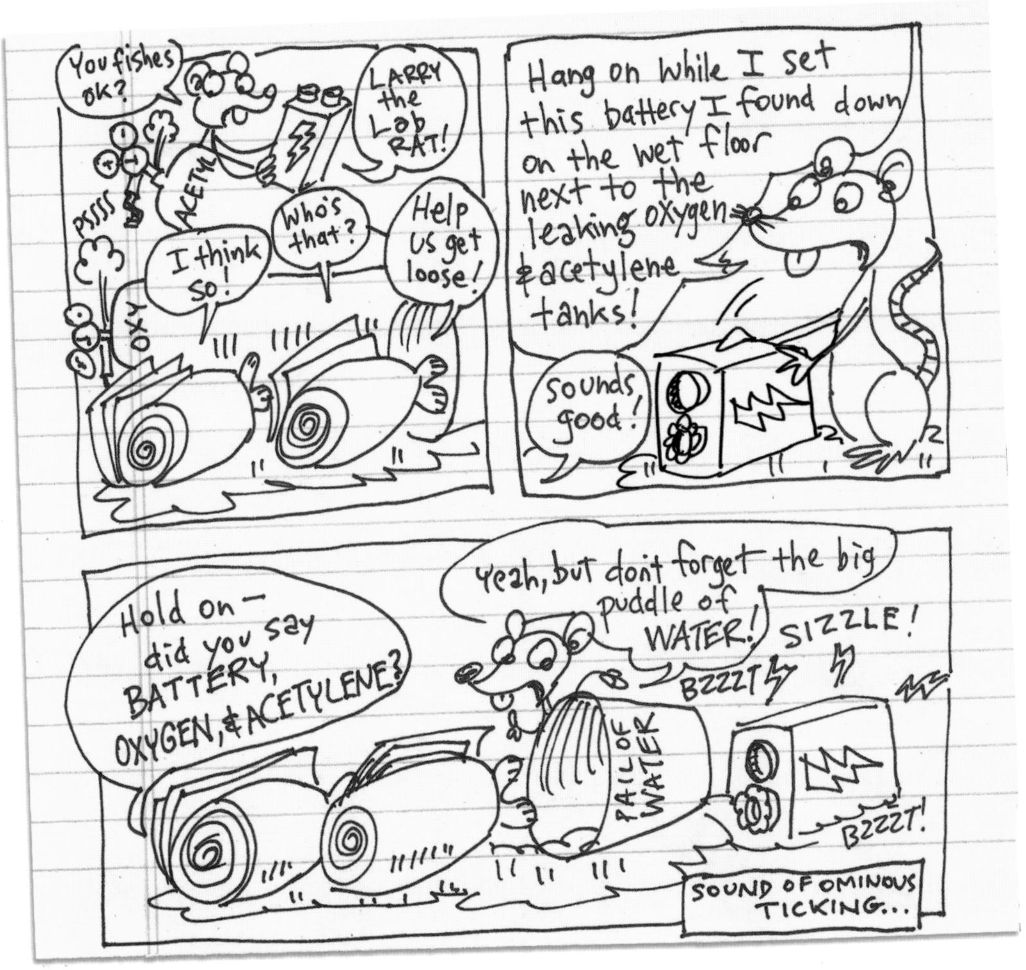
You fishes ok?
LARRY the Lab RAT!
ACETYL
PSSSS
OXY
I think so!
Who's that?
Help us get loose!
Hang on while I set this battery I found down on the wet floor next to the leaking oxygen & acetylene tanks!
Sounds good!
Hold on — did you say BATTERY, OXYGEN, & ACETYLENE?
Yeah, but don't forget the big puddle of WATER!
SIZZLE!
BZZZT
PAIL OF WATER
BZZZT!
SOUND OF OMINOUS TICKING...

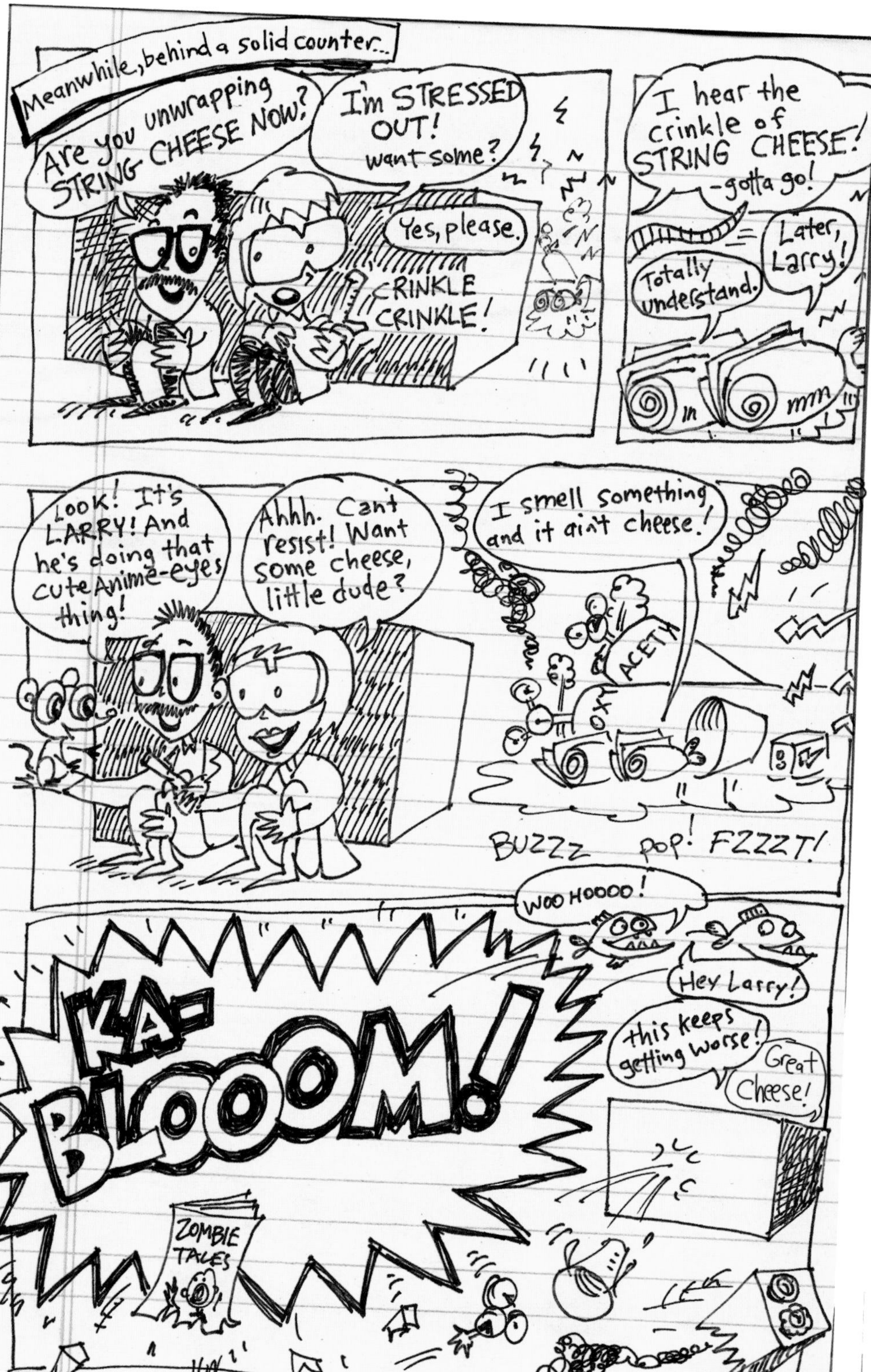

Meanwhile, behind a solid counter...
Are you unwrapping STRING CHEESE NOW?
I'm STRESSED OUT! want some?
Yes, please.
CRINKLE CRINKLE!
I hear the crinkle of STRING CHEESE! -gotta go!
Totally understand.
Later, Larry!
Look! It's LARRY! And he's doing that cute Anime-eyes thing!
Ahhh. Can't resist! Want some cheese, little dude?
I smell something and it ain't cheese!
ACETY
OXY
BUZZz pop! FZZZT!
WOO HOOOO!
Hey Larry!
this keeps getting worse!
Great Cheese!
KA-BLOOOM!
ZOMBIE TALES

oh no! they landed in the ROBOTICS LAB!
I know! I can read!
Any more cheese?
ROBOTICS LAB
CRASH!
we should go look.
Yes
You first?
NO
You want ME to go first?
Yes
BASH!
SNAP! SNAP!
No
GNASH! GNASH!
SNAP!

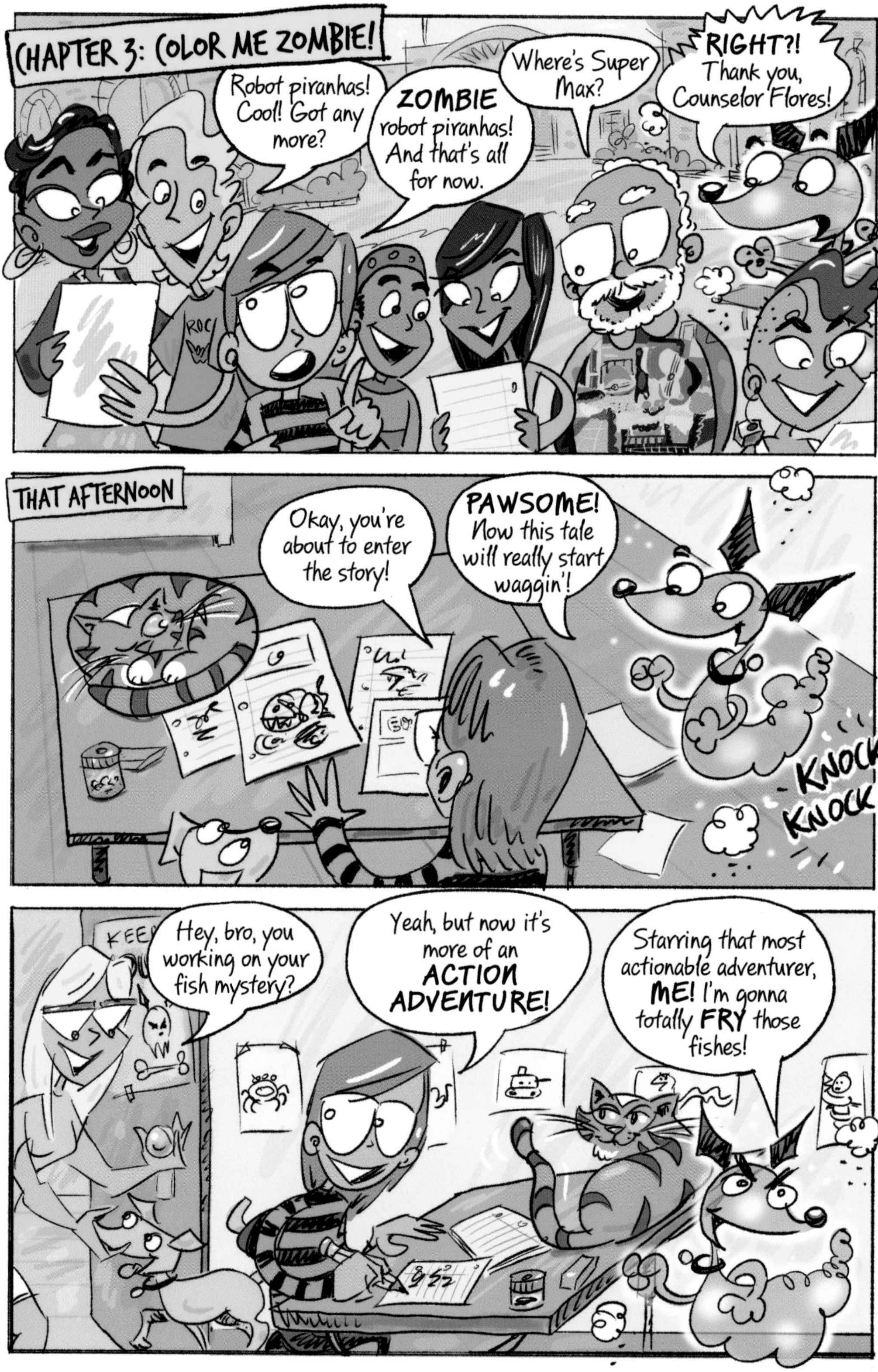
CHAPTER 3: COLOR ME ZOMBIE!
Robot piranhas! Cool! Got any more?
ZOMBIE robot piranhas! And that's all for now.
Where's Super Max?
RIGHT?! Thank you, Counselor Flores!
THAT AFTERNOON
Okay, you're about to enter the story!
PAWSOME! Now this tale will really start waggin'!
KNOCK KNOCK!
Hey, bro, you working on your fish mystery?
Yeah, but now it's more of an ACTION ADVENTURE!
Starring that most actionable adventurer, ME! I'm gonna totally FRY those fishes!

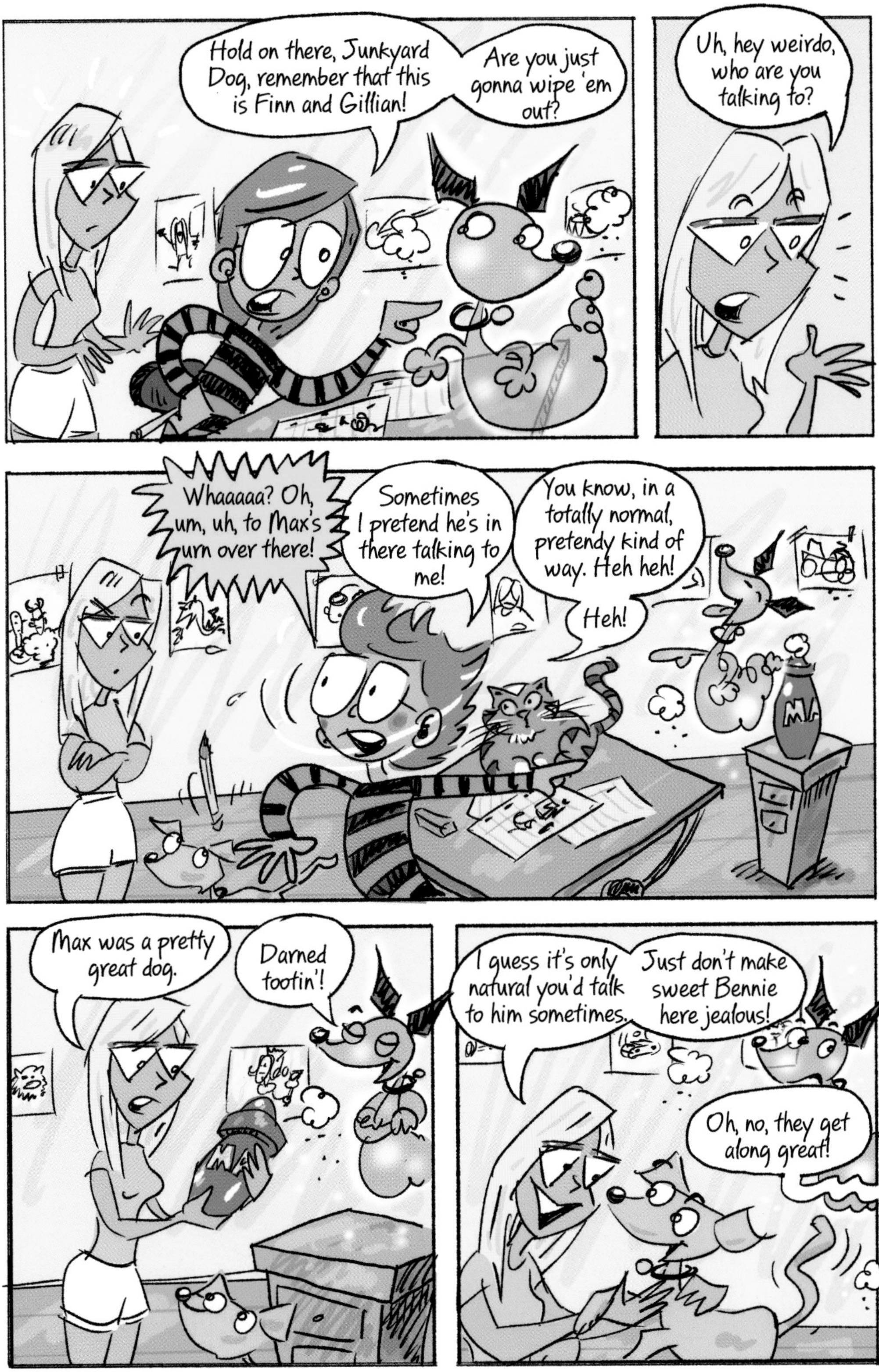
Hold on there, Junkyard Dog, remember that this is Finn and Gillian!
Are you just gonna wipe 'em out?
Uh, hey weirdo, who are you talking to?
Whaaaaa? Oh, um, uh, to Max's urn over there!
Sometimes I pretend he's in there talking to me!
You know, in a totally normal, pretendy kind of way. Heh heh!
Heh!
Max was a pretty great dog.
Darned tootin'!
I guess it's only natural you'd talk to him sometimes.
Just don't make sweet Bennie here jealous!
Oh, no, they get along great!

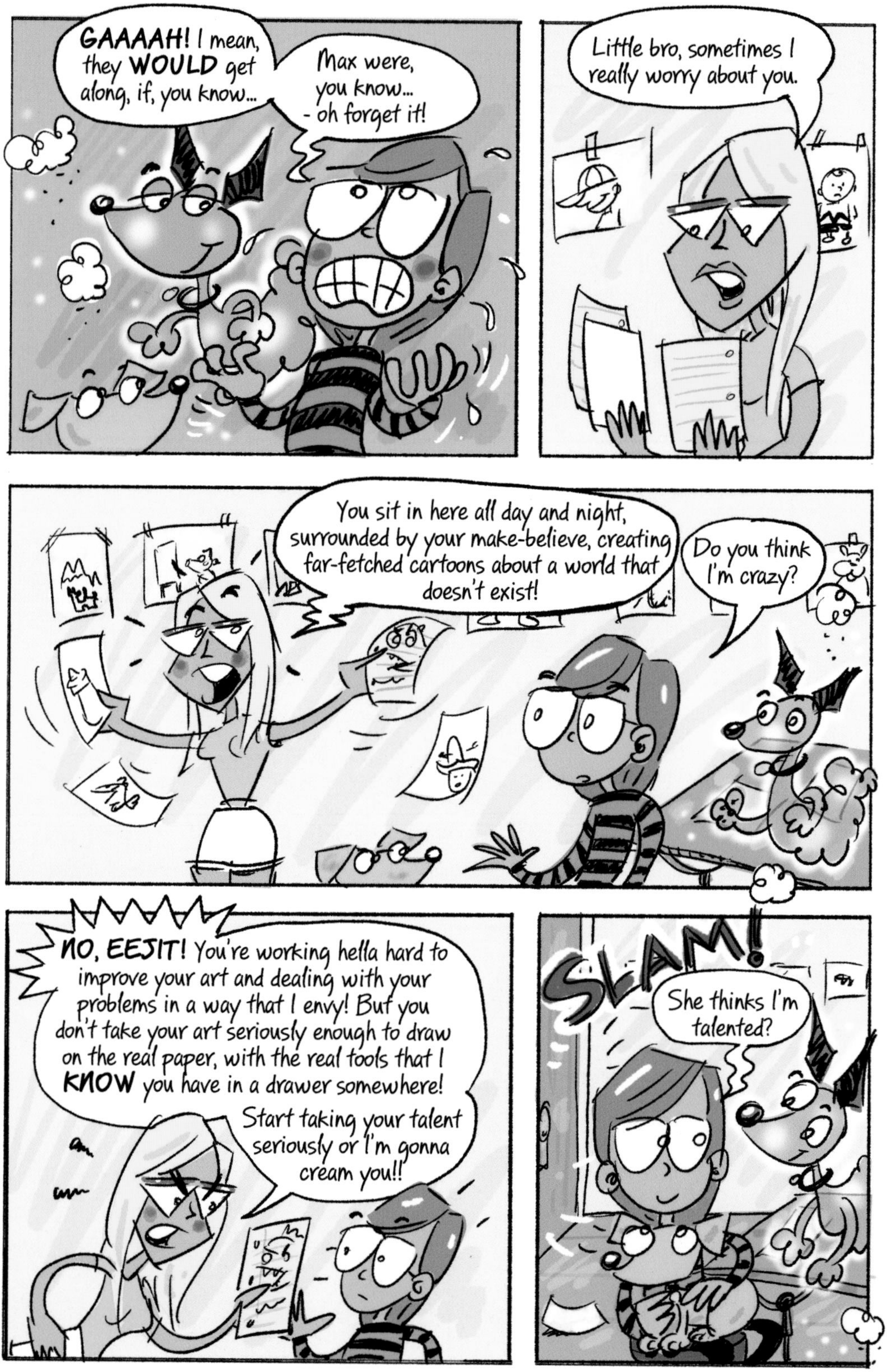
GAAAAH! I mean, they WOULD get along, if, you know...
Max were, you know... - oh forget it!
Little bro, sometimes I really worry about you.
You sit in here all day and night, surrounded by your make-believe, creating far-fetched cartoons about a world that doesn't exist!
Do you think I'm crazy?
NO, EEJIT! You're working hella hard to improve your art and dealing with your problems in a way that I envy! But you don't take your art seriously enough to draw on the real paper, with the real tools that I KNOW you have in a drawer somewhere!
Start taking your talent seriously or I'm gonna cream you!!
SLAM!
She thinks I'm talented?

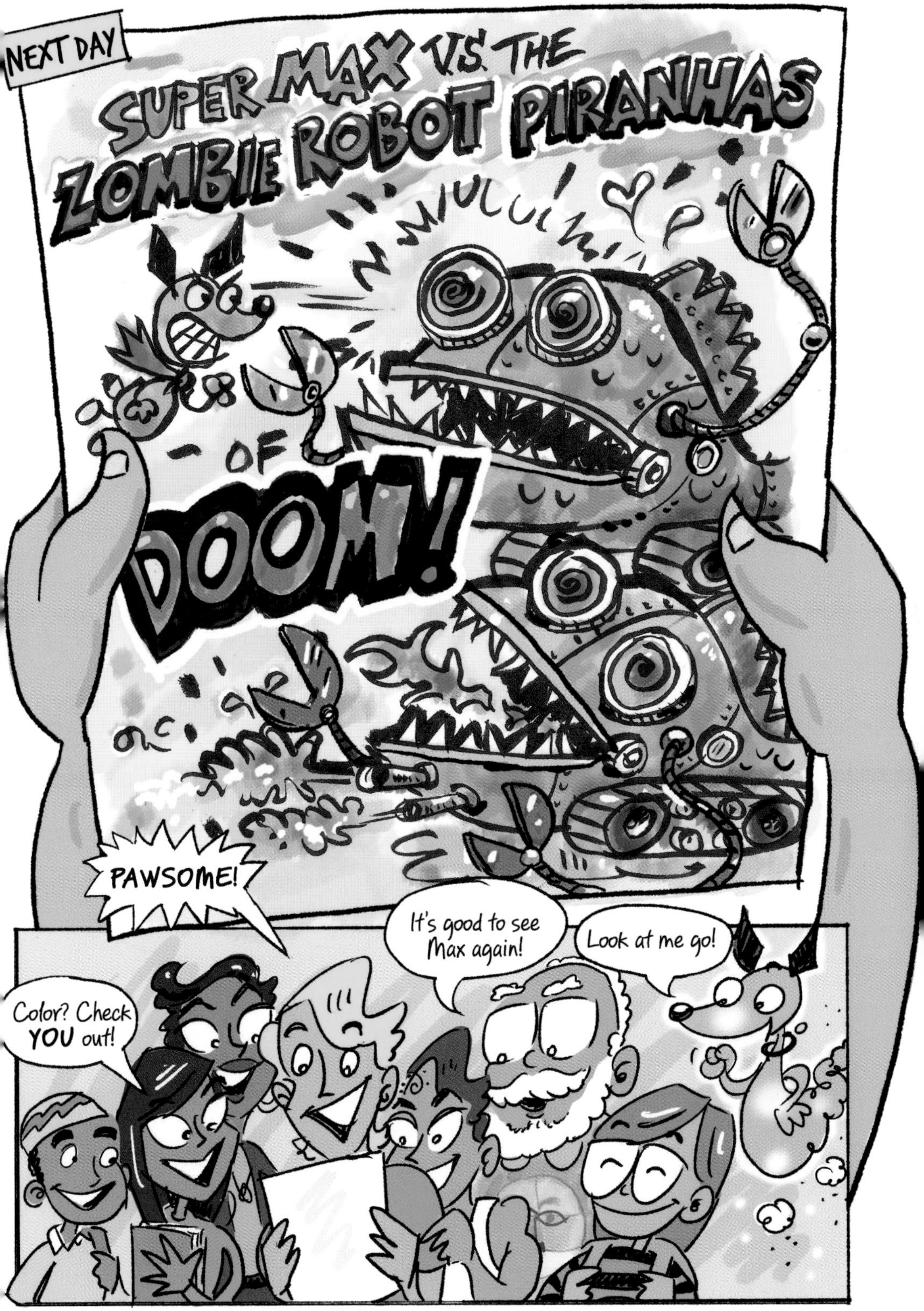
NEXT DAY
SUPER MAX VS. THE ZOMBIE ROBOT PIRANHAS
OF
DOOM!
PAWSOME!
Color? Check YOU out!
It's good to see Max again!
Look at me go!

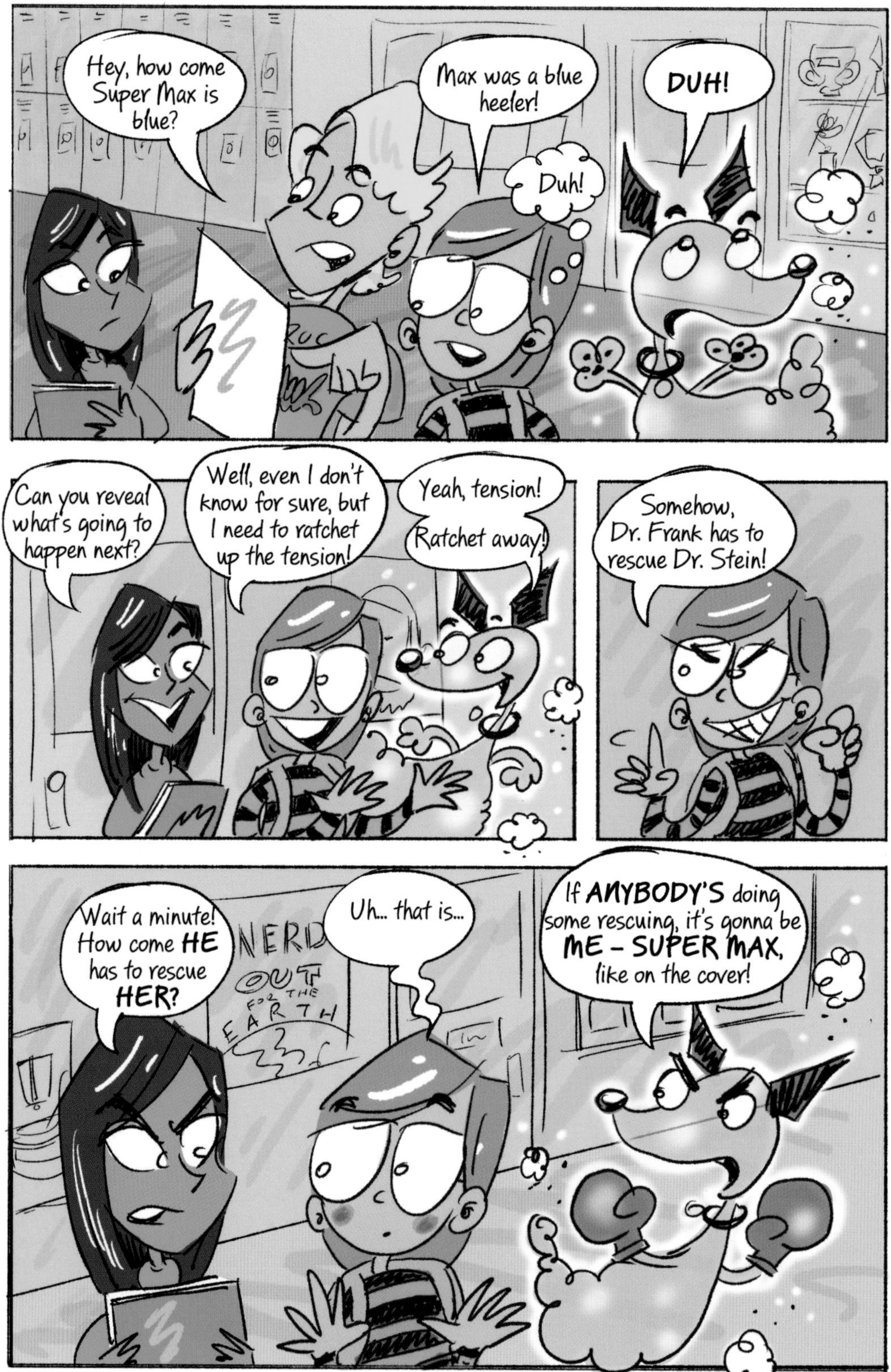
Hey, how come Super Max is blue?
Max was a blue heeler!
Duh!
DUH!
Can you reveal what's going to happen next?
Well, even I don't know for sure, but I need to ratchet up the tension!
Yeah, tension!
Ratchet away!
Somehow, Dr. Frank has to rescue Dr. Stein!
Wait a minute! How come HE has to rescue HER?
NERD
OUT FOR THE EARTH
Uh... that is...
If ANYBODY'S doing some rescuing, it's gonna be ME – SUPER MAX, like on the cover!

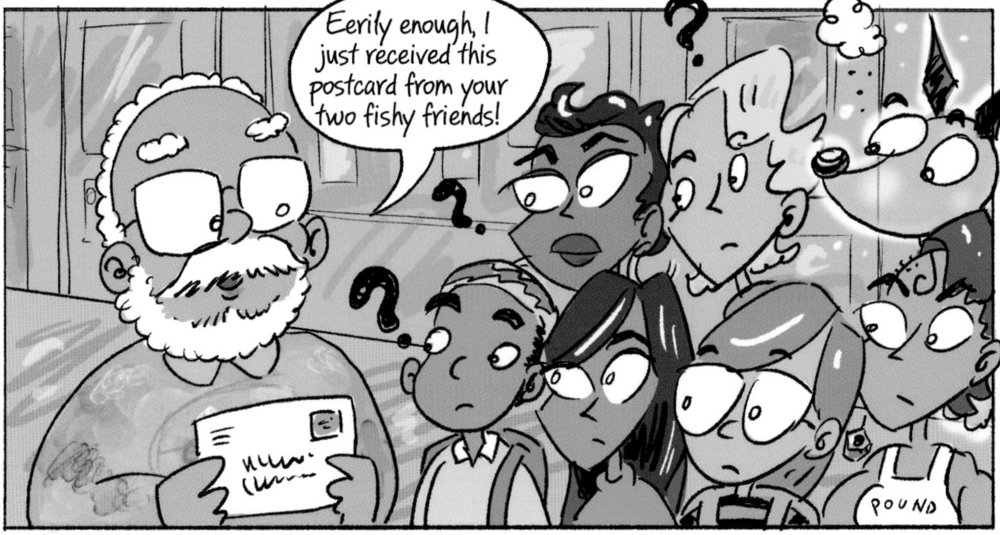
Eerily enough, I just received this postcard from your two fishy friends!
POUND

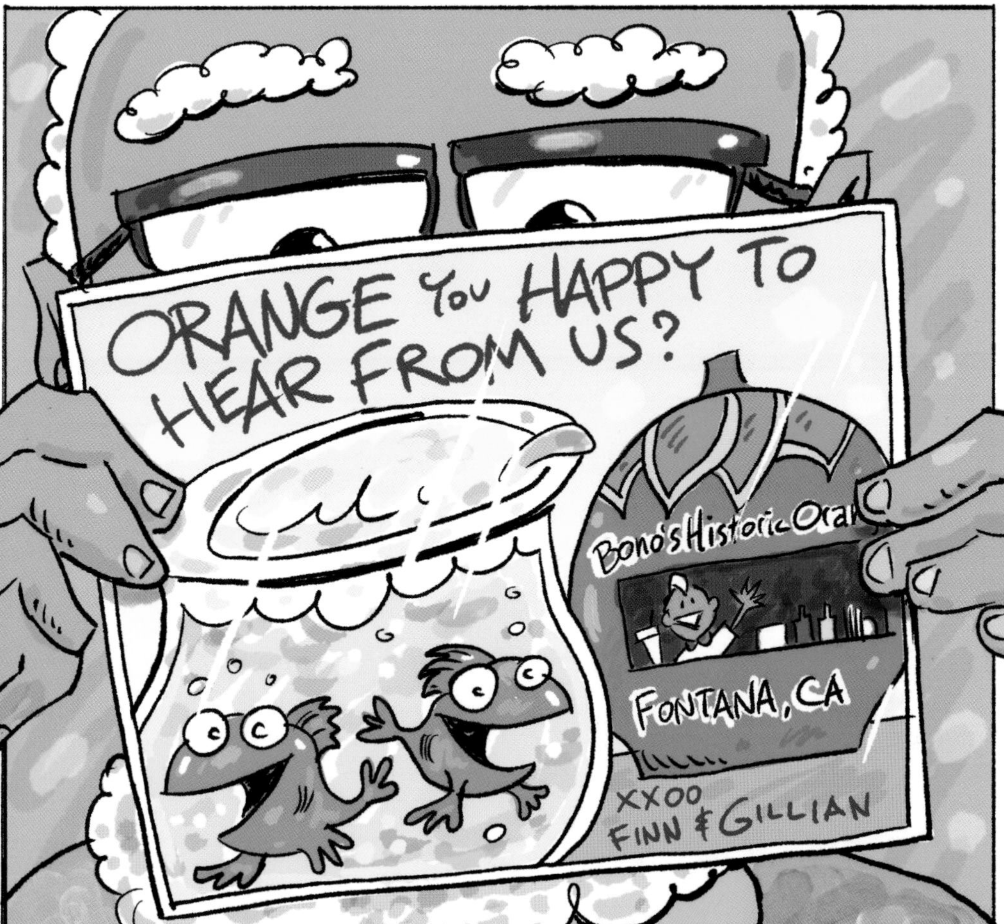
ORANGE YOU HAPPY TO HEAR FROM US?
Bono's Historic Oran
FONTANA, CA
XXOO
FINN & GILLIAN

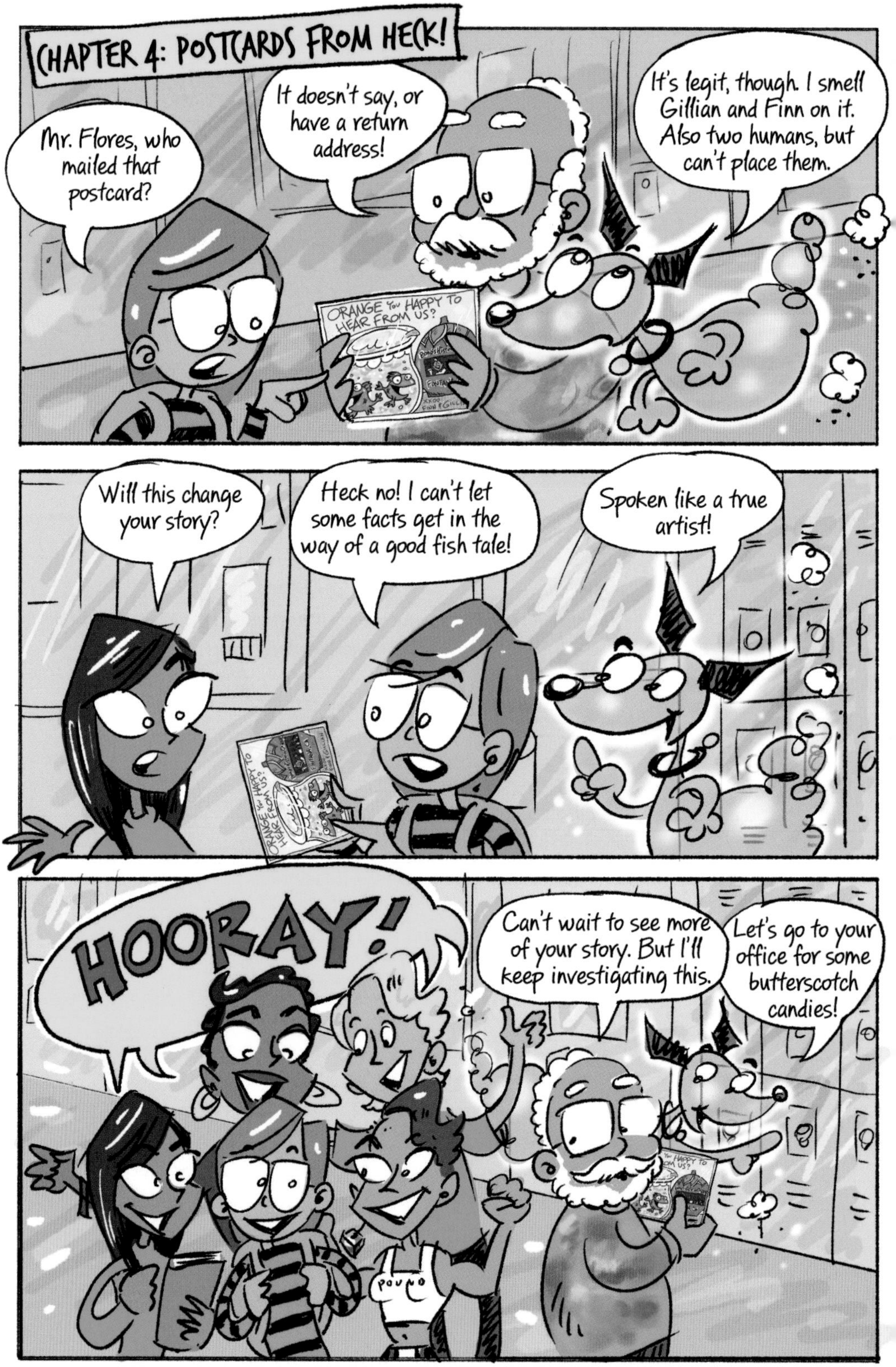
CHAPTER 4: POSTCARDS FROM HECK!
Mr. Flores, who mailed that postcard?
It doesn't say, or have a return address!
It's legit, though. I smell Gillian and Finn on it. Also two humans, but can't place them.
ORANGE You HAPPY TO HEAR FROM US?
Will this change your story?
Heck no! I can't let some facts get in the way of a good fish tale!
Spoken like a true artist!
HOORAY!
Can't wait to see more of your story. But I'll keep investigating this.
Let's go to your office for some butterscotch candies!
POUND

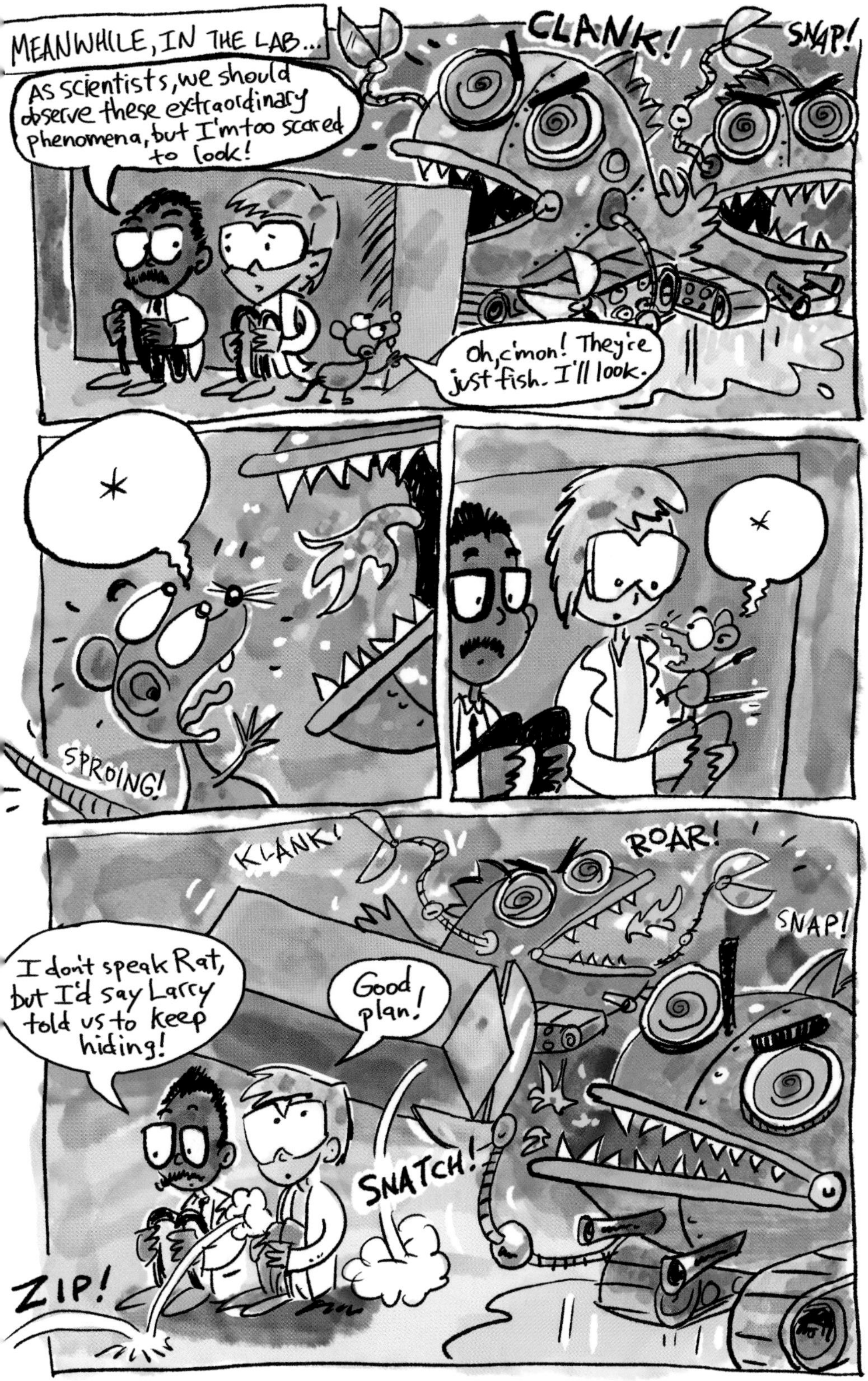
MEANWHILE, IN THE LAB...
As scientists, we should observe these extraordinary phenomena, but I'm too scared to look!
CLANK!
SNAP!
Oh, c'mon! They're just fish. I'll look.
*
SPROING!
*
KLANK!
ROAR!
SNAP!
I don't speak Rat, but I'd say Larry told us to keep hiding!
Good plan!
SNATCH!
ZIP!

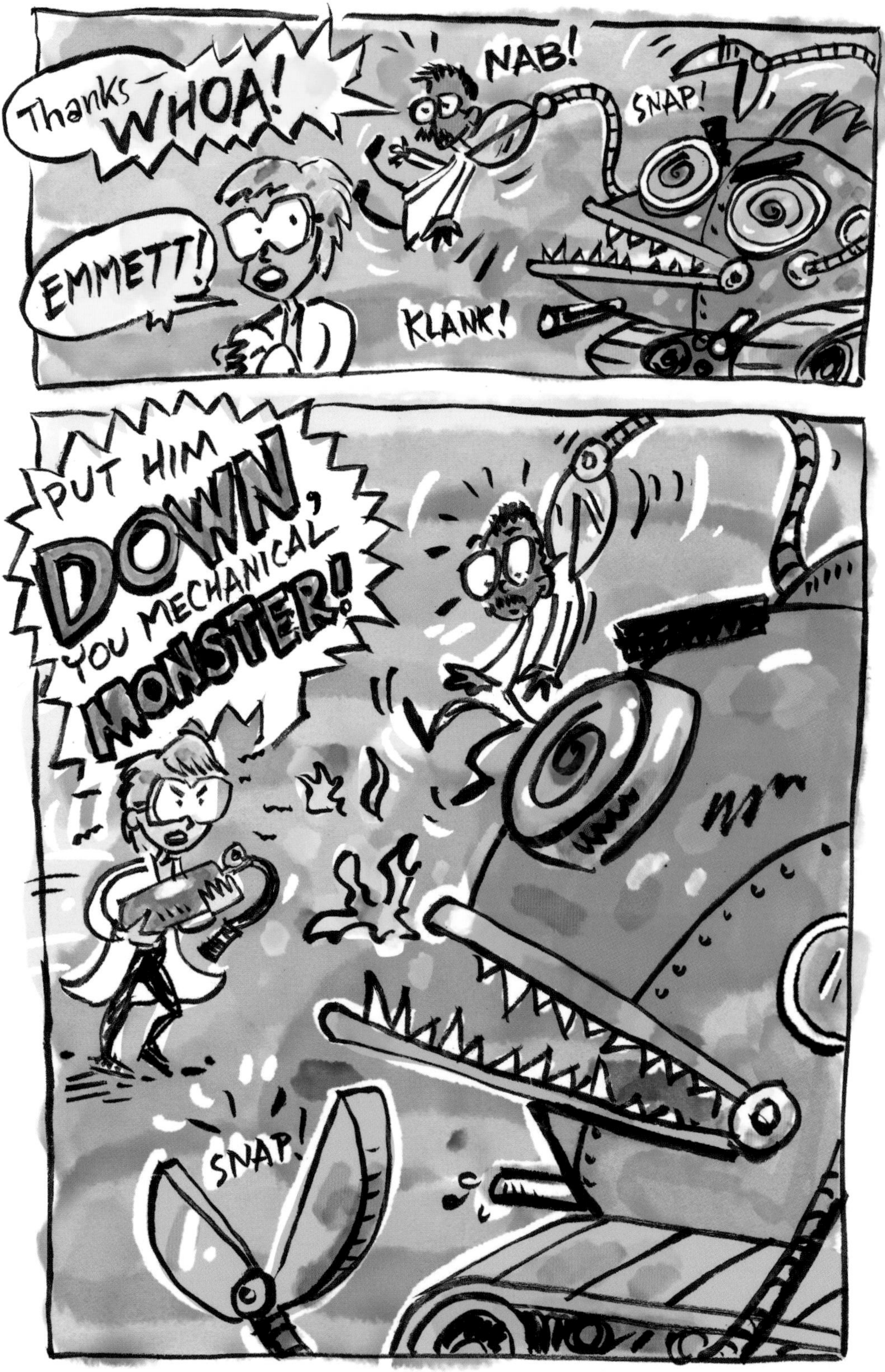
Thanks—WHOA!
NAB!
SNAP!
EMMETT!
KLANK!
PUT HIM DOWN, YOU MECHANICAL MONSTER!
SNAP!

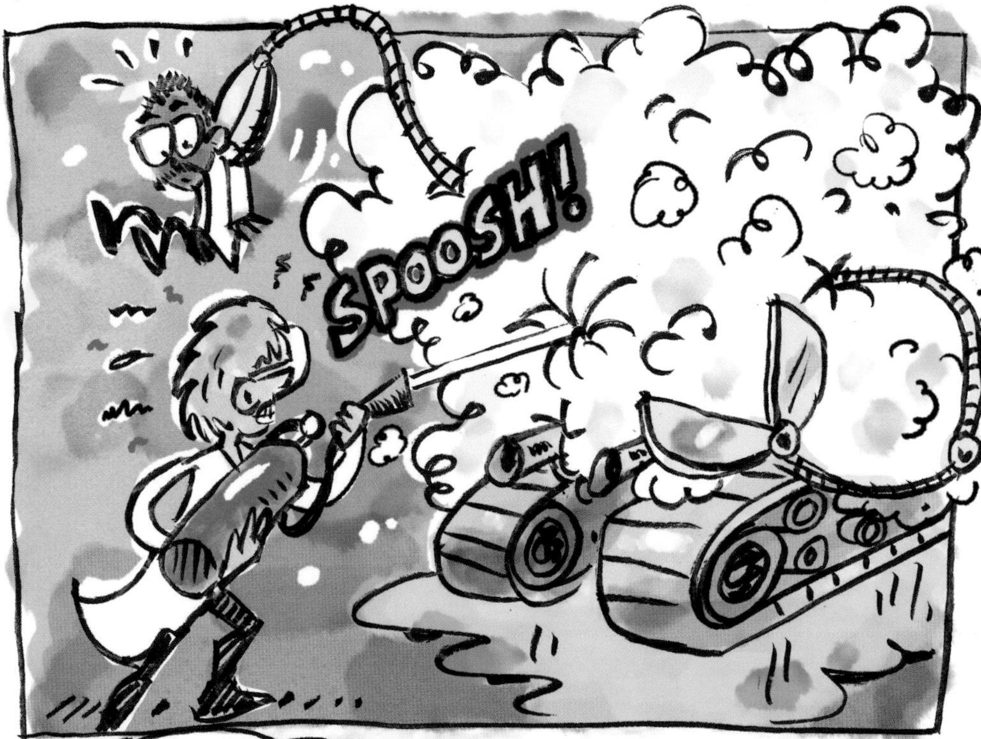
SPOOSH!

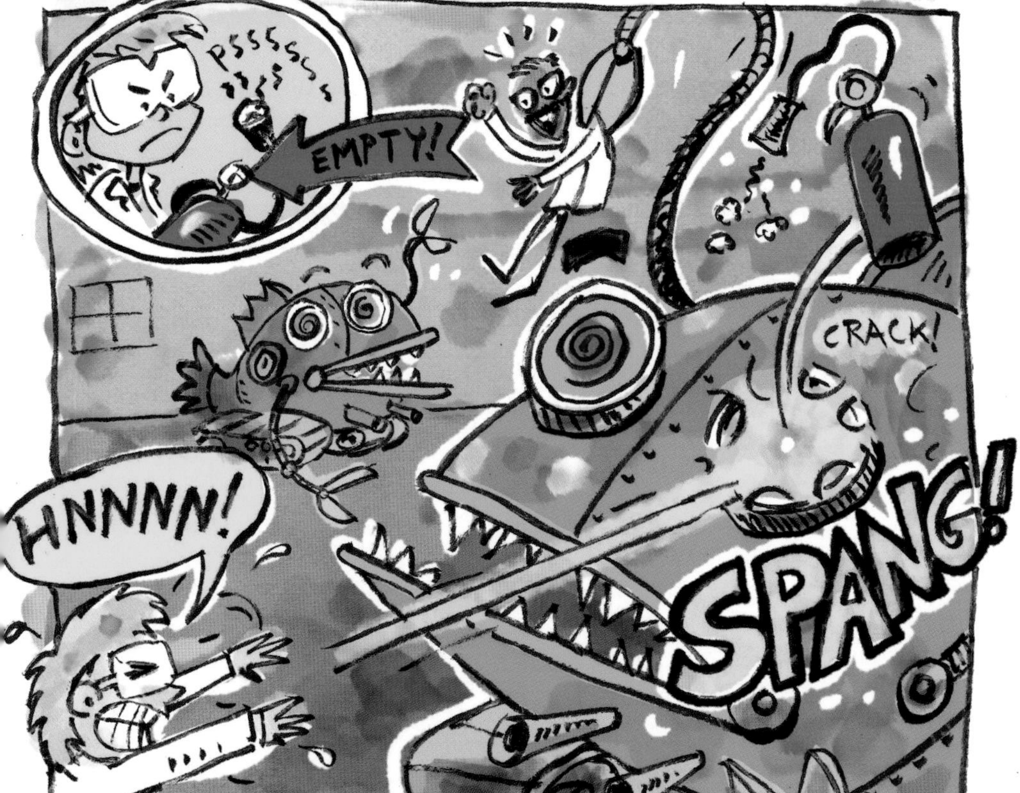
PSSSSSSS
EMPTY!
CRACK!
HNNNN!
SPANG!

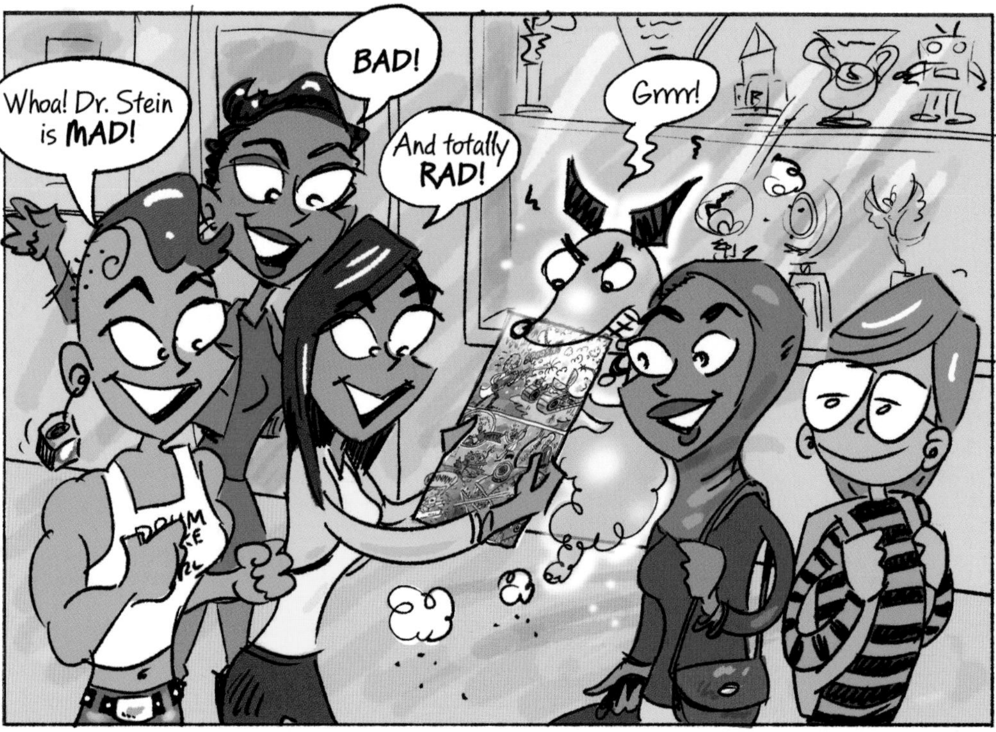
Whoa! Dr. Stein is MAD!
BAD!
And totally RAD!
Grrr!

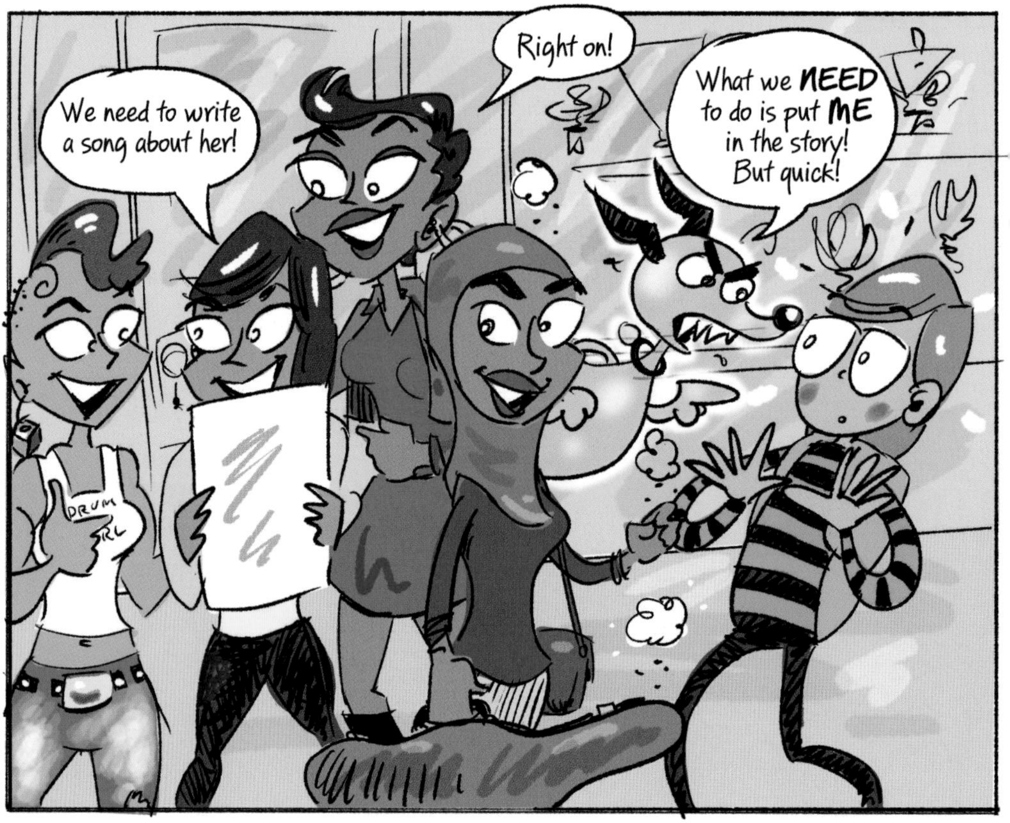
We need to write a song about her!
Right on!
What we NEED to do is put ME in the story! But quick!

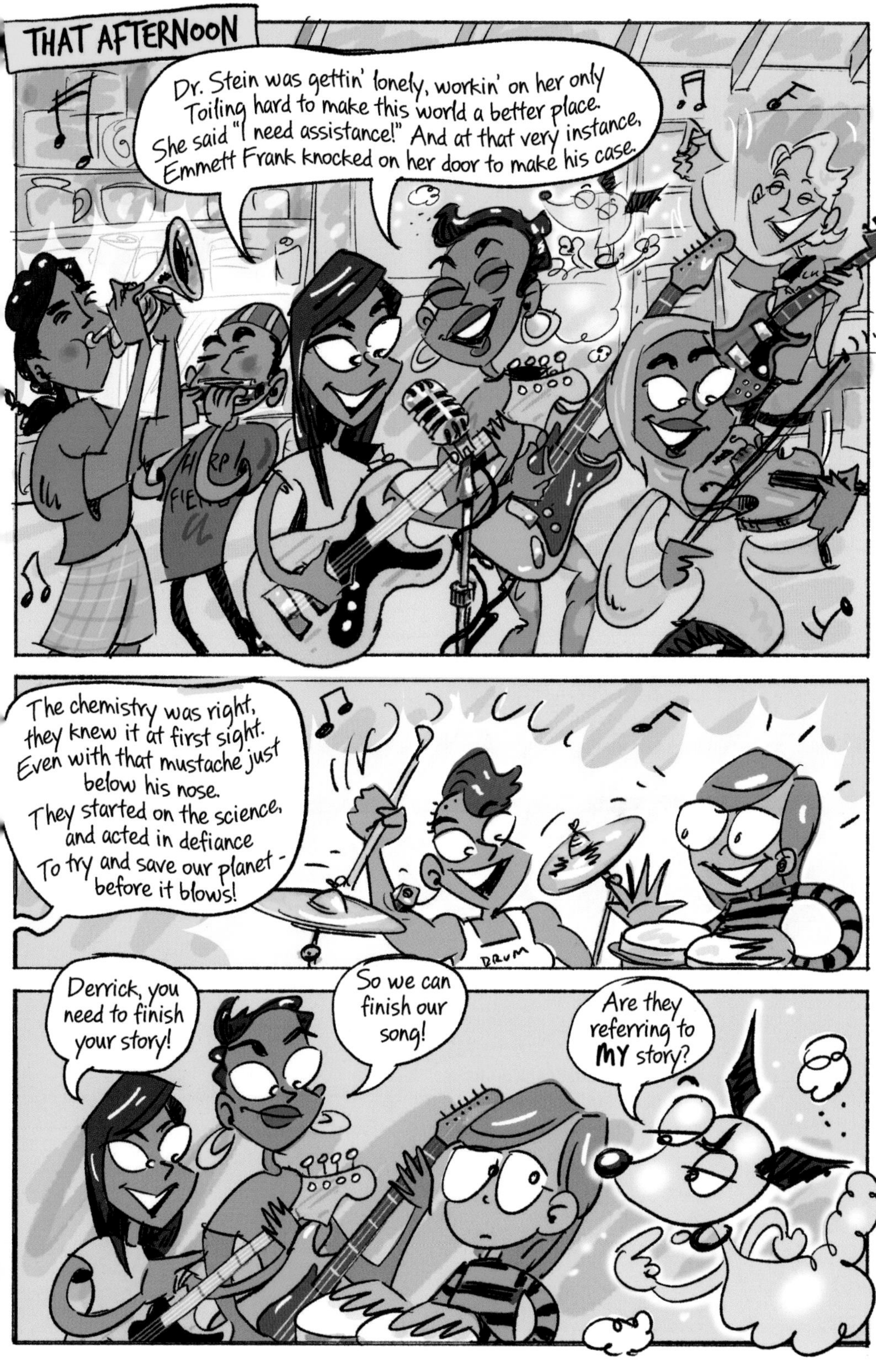
THAT AFTERNOON
Dr. Stein was gettin' lonely, workin' on her only Toiling hard to make this world a better place. She said "I need assistance!" And at that very instance, Emmett Frank knocked on her door to make his case.
The chemistry was right, they knew it at first sight. Even with that mustache just below his nose. They started on the science, and acted in defiance To try and save our planet - before it blows!
DRUM
Derrick, you need to finish your story!
So we can finish our song!
Are they referring to MY story?

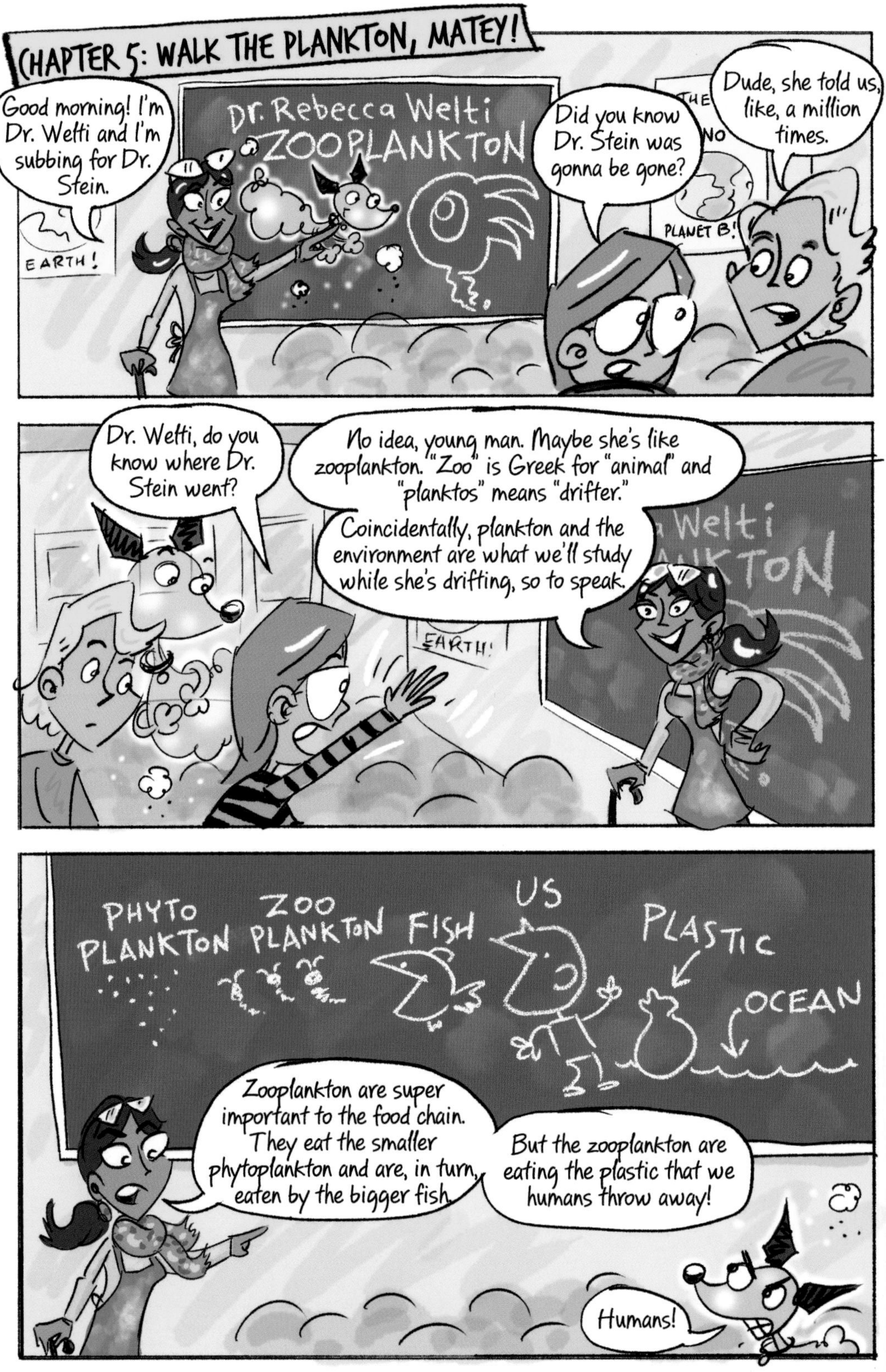

CHAPTER 5: WALK THE PLANKTON, MATEY!
Good morning! I'm Dr. Welti and I'm subbing for Dr. Stein.
Dr. Rebecca Welti ZOOPLANKTON
EARTH!
Did you know Dr. Stein was gonna be gone?
Dude, she told us, like, a million times.
PLANET B!
Dr. Welti, do you know where Dr. Stein went?
No idea, young man. Maybe she's like zooplankton. "Zoo" is Greek for "animal" and "planktos" means "drifter."
Coincidentally, plankton and the environment are what we'll study while she's drifting, so to speak.
EARTH!
PHYTO PLANKTON
ZOO PLANKTON
FISH
US
PLASTIC
OCEAN
Zooplankton are super important to the food chain. They eat the smaller phytoplankton and are, in turn, eaten by the bigger fish.
But the zooplankton are eating the plastic that we humans throw away!
Humans!

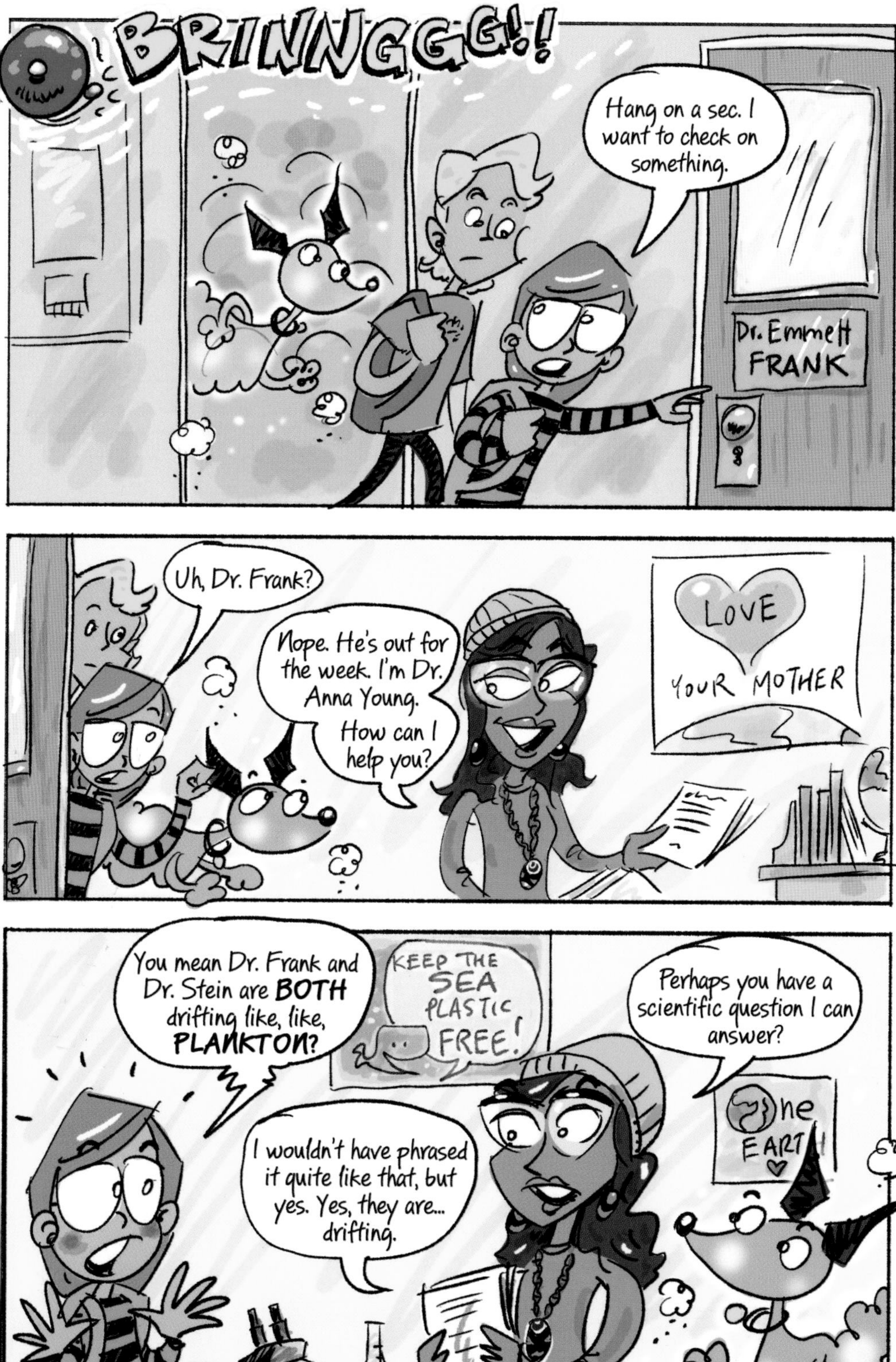
BRINNGGG!!
Hang on a sec. I want to check on something.
Dr. Emmett FRANK
Uh, Dr. Frank?
Nope. He's out for the week. I'm Dr. Anna Young.
How can I help you?
LOVE YOUR MOTHER
You mean Dr. Frank and Dr. Stein are **BOTH** drifting like, like, **PLANKTON?**
KEEP THE SEA PLASTIC FREE!
Perhaps you have a scientific question I can answer?
I wouldn't have phrased it quite like that, but yes. Yes, they are... drifting.
One EARTH

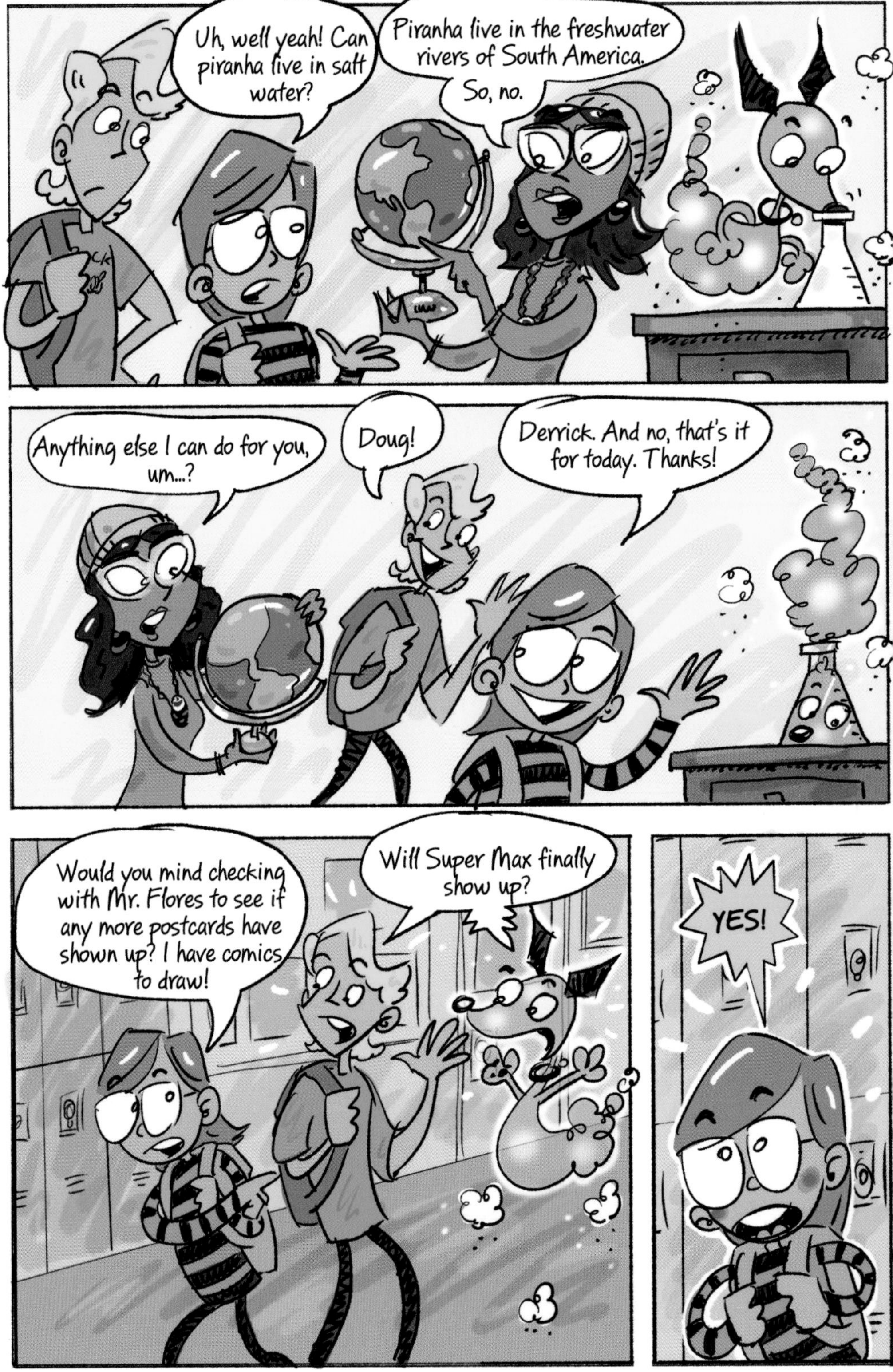
Uh, well yeah! Can piranha live in salt water?
Piranha live in the freshwater rivers of South America.
So, no.
Anything else I can do for you, um...?
Doug!
Derrick. And no, that's it for today. Thanks!
Would you mind checking with Mr. Flores to see if any more postcards have shown up? I have comics to draw!
Will Super Max finally show up?
YES!

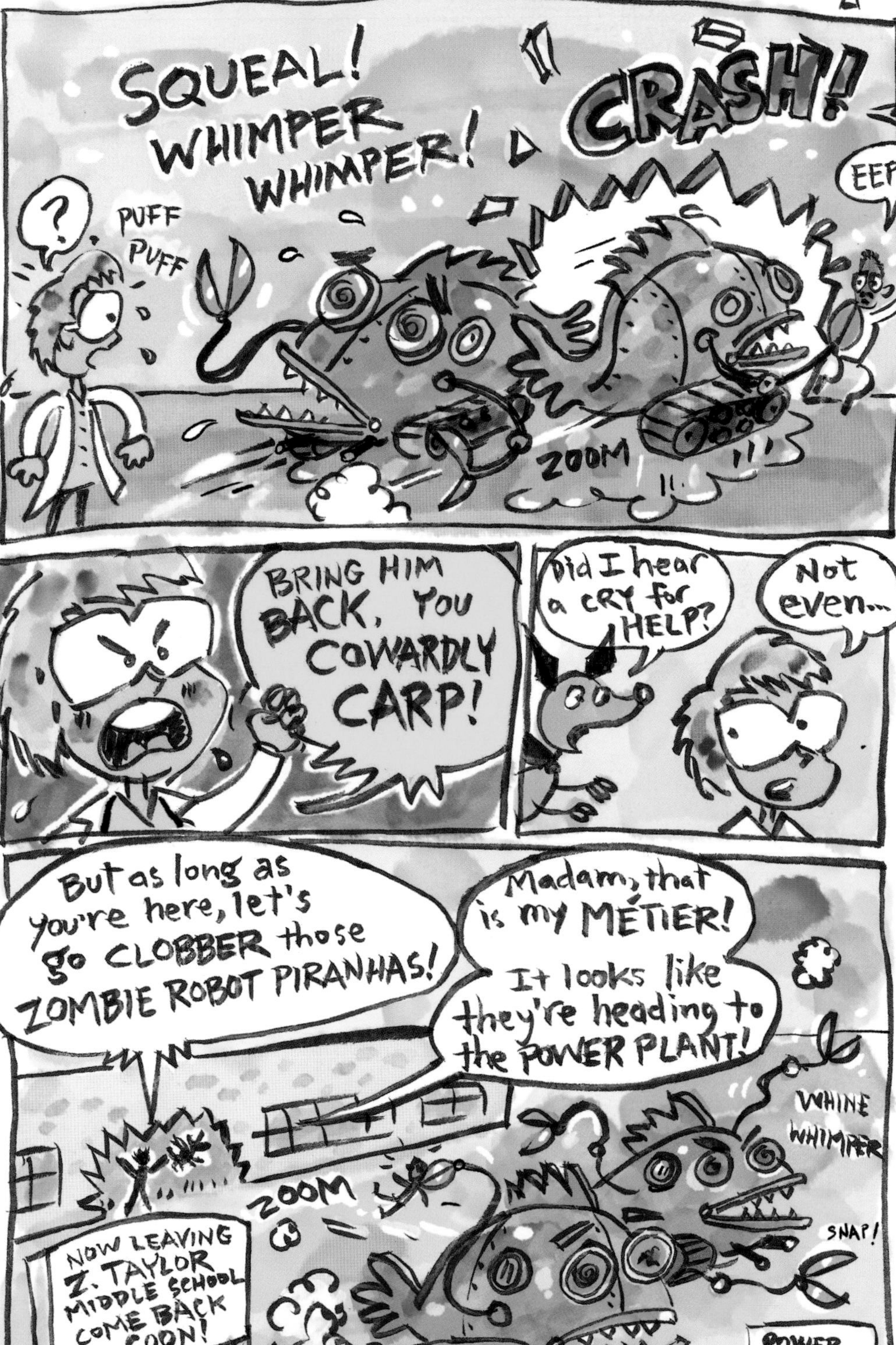
SQUEAL! WHIMPER WHIMPER!
CRASH!
?
PUFF PUFF
EEP!
ZOOM
BRING HIM BACK, YOU COWARDLY CARP!
Did I hear a cry for HELP?
Not even...
But as long as you're here, let's go CLOBBER those ZOMBIE ROBOT PIRANHAS!
Madam, that is my MÉTIER!
It looks like they're heading to the POWER PLANT!
WHINE WHIMPER
ZOOM
SNAP!
NOW LEAVING Z. TAYLOR MIDDLE SCHOOL COME BACK SOON!
POWER PLANT

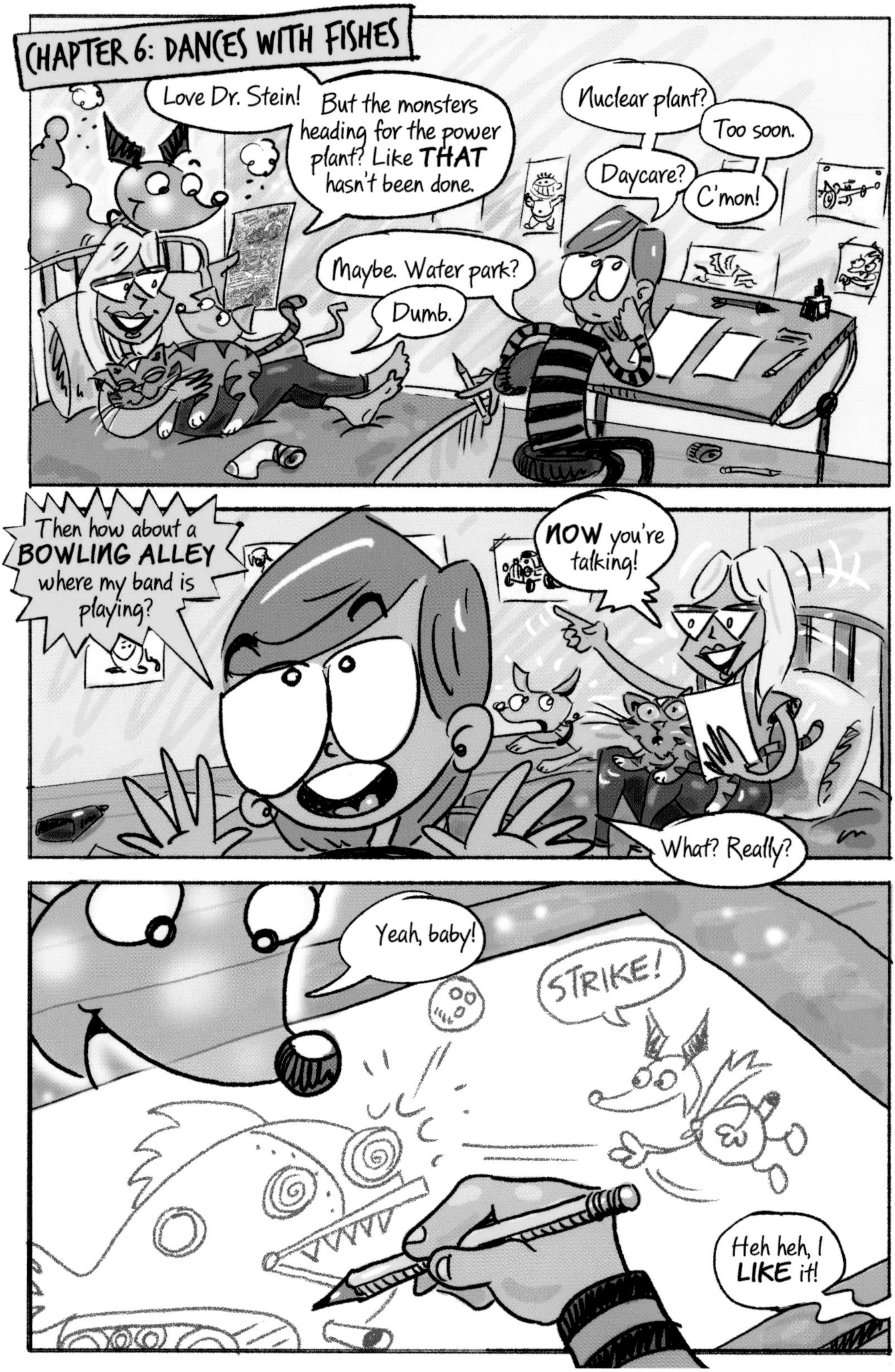
CHAPTER 6: DANCES WITH FISHES
Love Dr. Stein!
But the monsters heading for the power plant? Like THAT hasn't been done.
Nuclear plant?
Too soon.
Daycare?
C'mon!
Maybe. Water park?
Dumb.
Then how about a BOWLING ALLEY where my band is playing?
NOW you're talking!
What? Really?
Yeah, baby!
STRIKE!
Heh heh, I LIKE it!

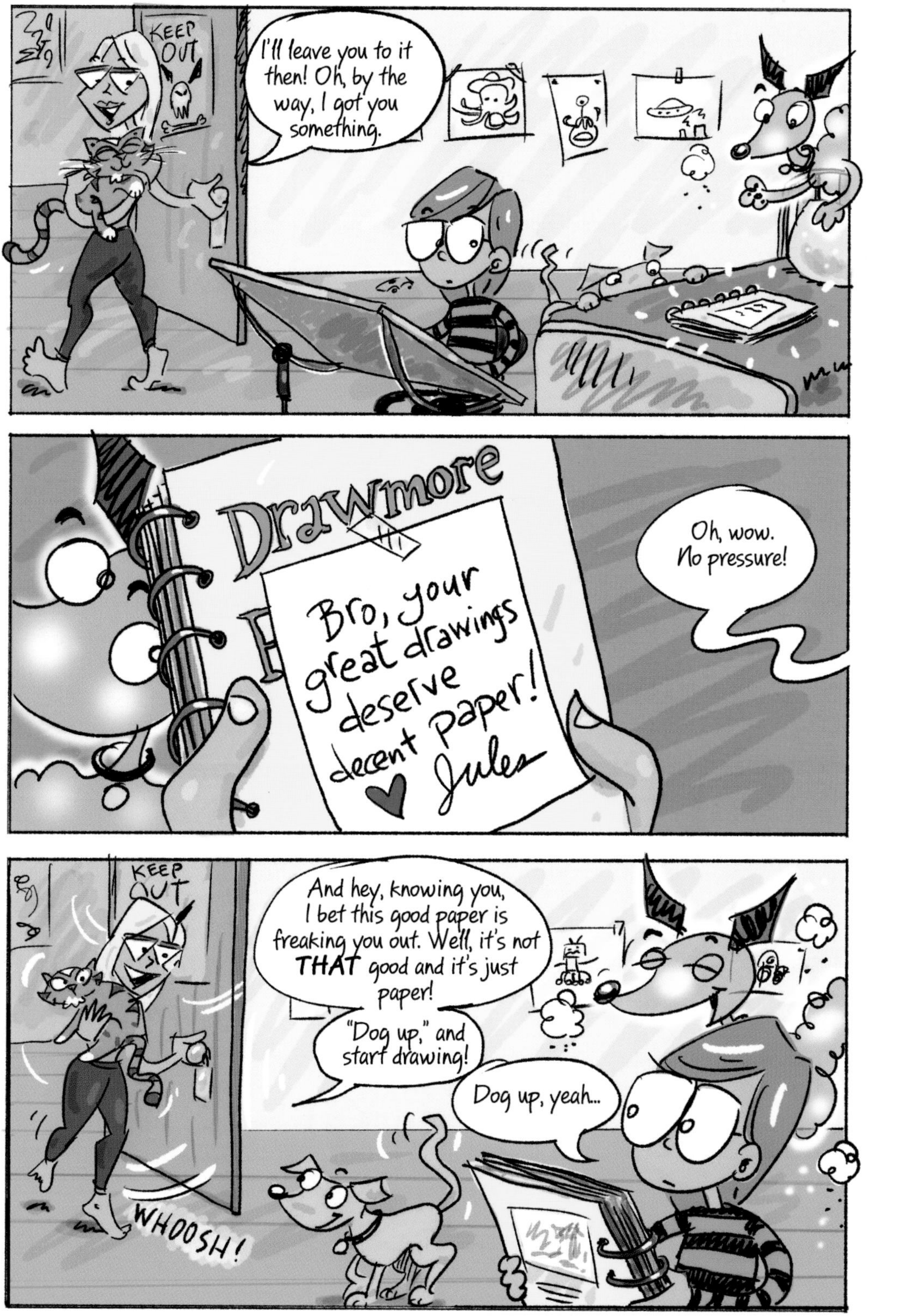

KEEP OUT
I'll leave you to it then! Oh, by the way, I got you something.
Drawmore
Bro, your great drawings deserve decent paper! Jules
Oh, wow. No pressure!
KEEP OUT
And hey, knowing you, I bet this good paper is freaking you out. Well, it's not **THAT** good and it's just paper!
"Dog up," and start drawing!
Dog up, yeah...
WHOOSH!

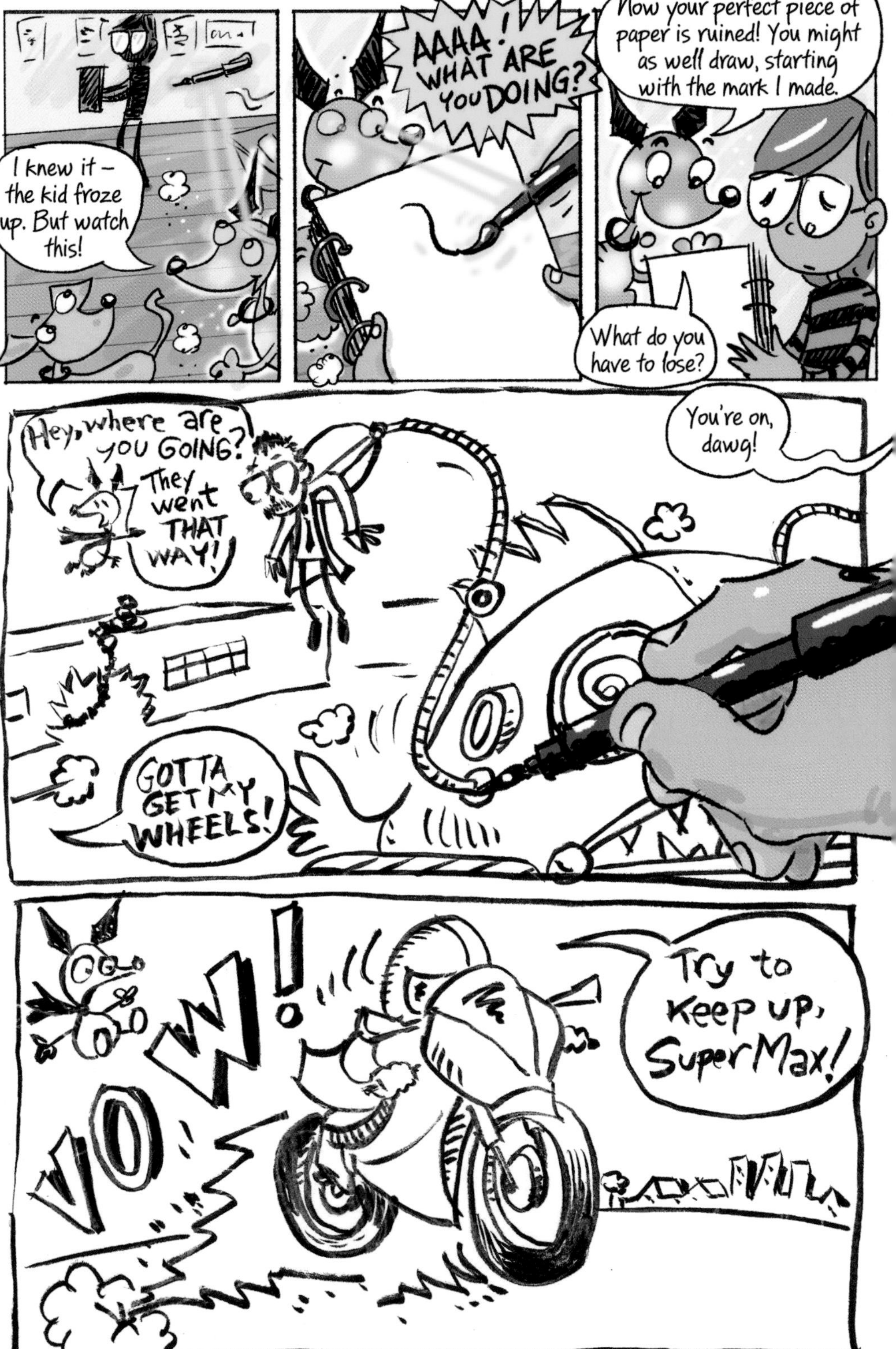
I knew it – the kid froze up. But watch this!
AAAA! WHAT ARE YOU DOING?
Now your perfect piece of paper is ruined! You might as well draw, starting with the mark I made.
What do you have to lose?
You're on, dawg!
Hey, where are you GOING?
They went THAT WAY!
GOTTA GET MY WHEELS!
VOOOW!
Try to keep up, SuperMax!

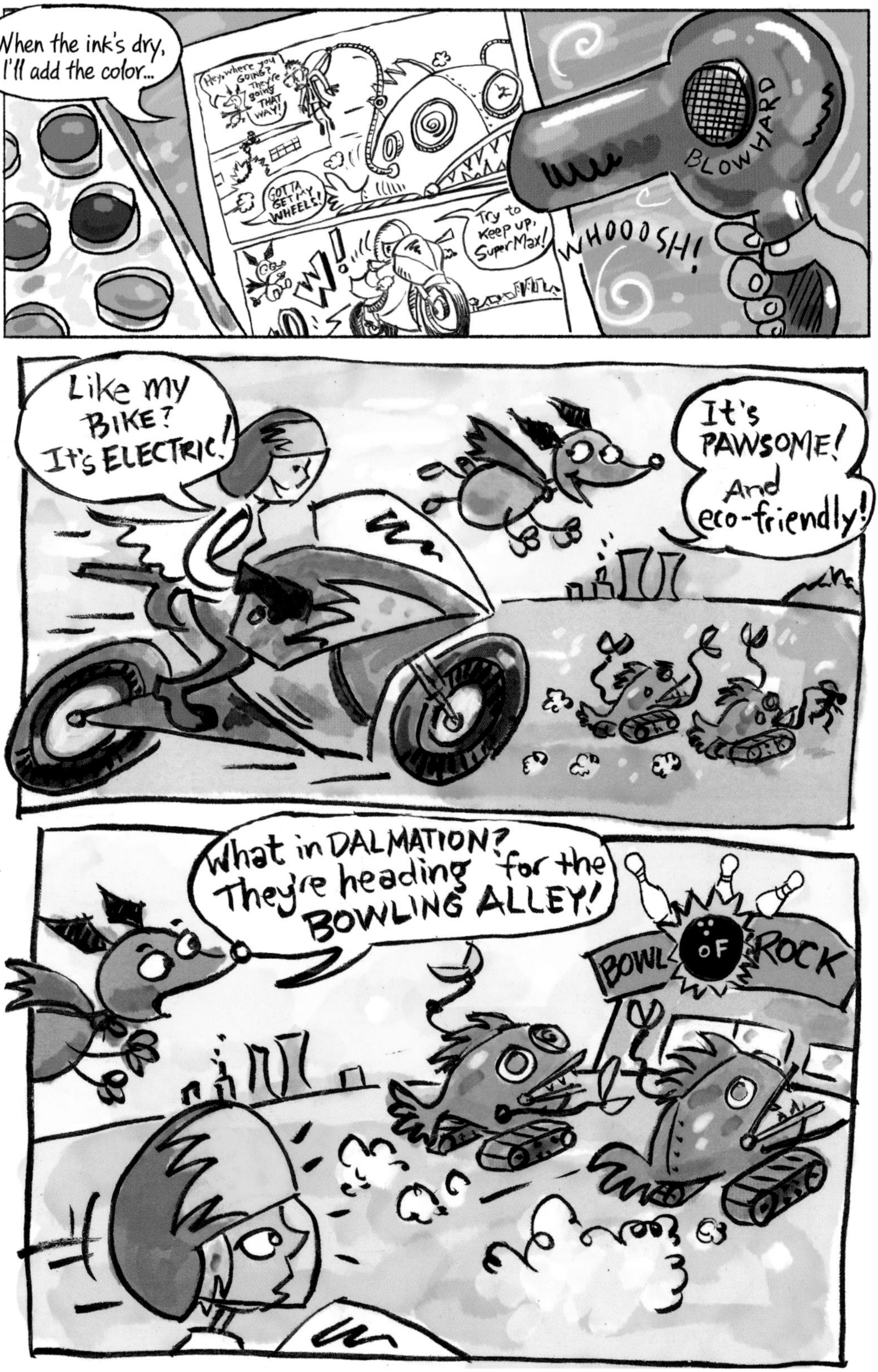
When the ink's dry, I'll add the color...
Hey, where you GOING? They're going THAT WAY!
GOTTA GET MY WHEELS!
Try to keep up, SuperMax!
WHOOOSH!
BLOWHARD
Like my BIKE? It's ELECTRIC!
It's PAWSOME! And eco-friendly!
What in DALMATION? They're heading for the BOWLING ALLEY!
BOWL OF ROCK

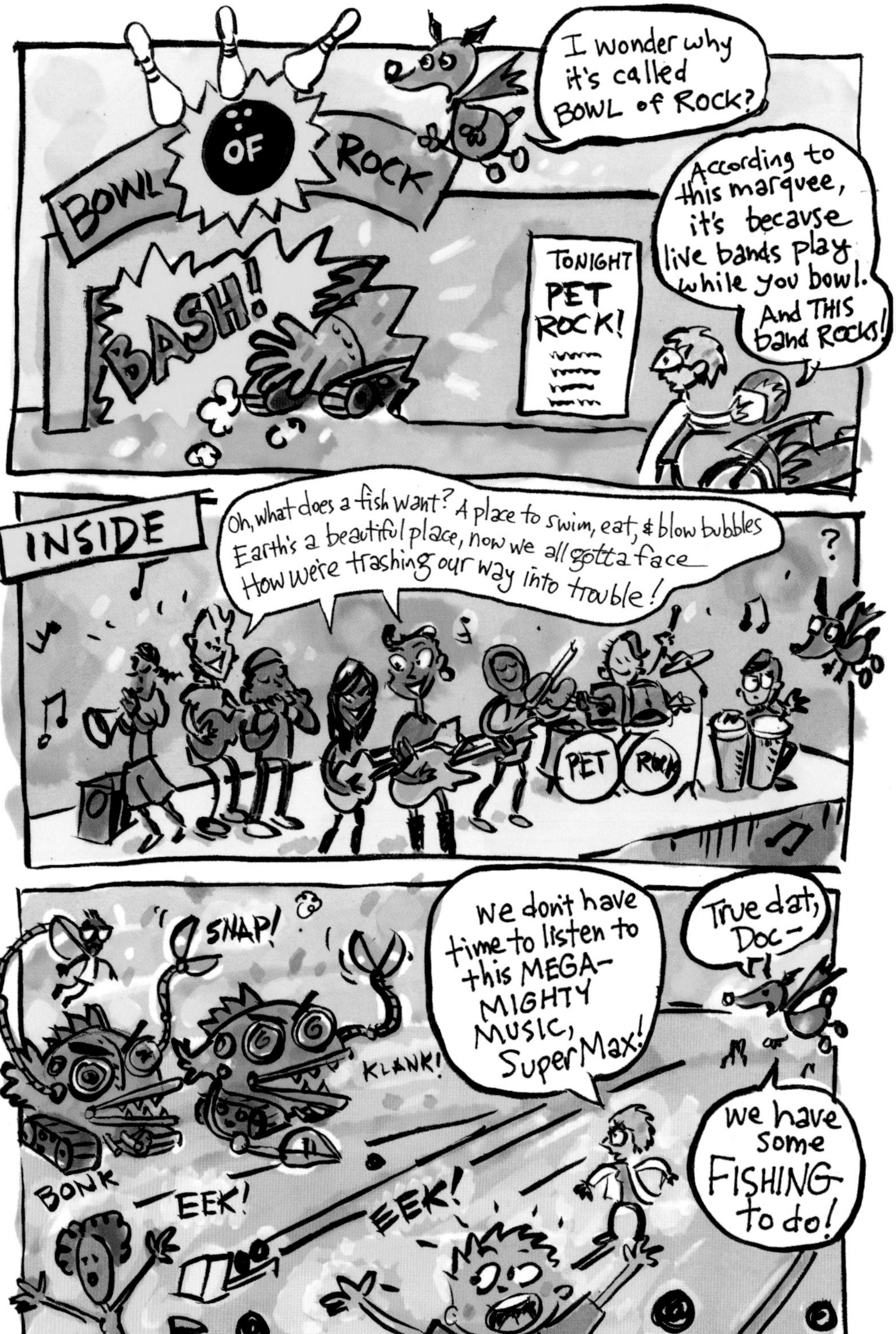
BOWL OF ROCK
I wonder why it's called BOWL of ROCK?
According to this marquee, it's because live bands play while you bowl.
And THIS band ROCKS!
TONIGHT PET ROCK!
BASH!
INSIDE
Oh, what does a fish want? A place to swim, eat, & blow bubbles
Earth's a beautiful place, now we all gotta face
How we're trashing our way into trouble!
PET ROCK
SNAP!
KLANK!
we don't have time to listen to this MEGA-MIGHTY MUSIC, SuperMax!
True dat, Doc–
we have some FISHING to do!
BONK
EEK!
EEK!

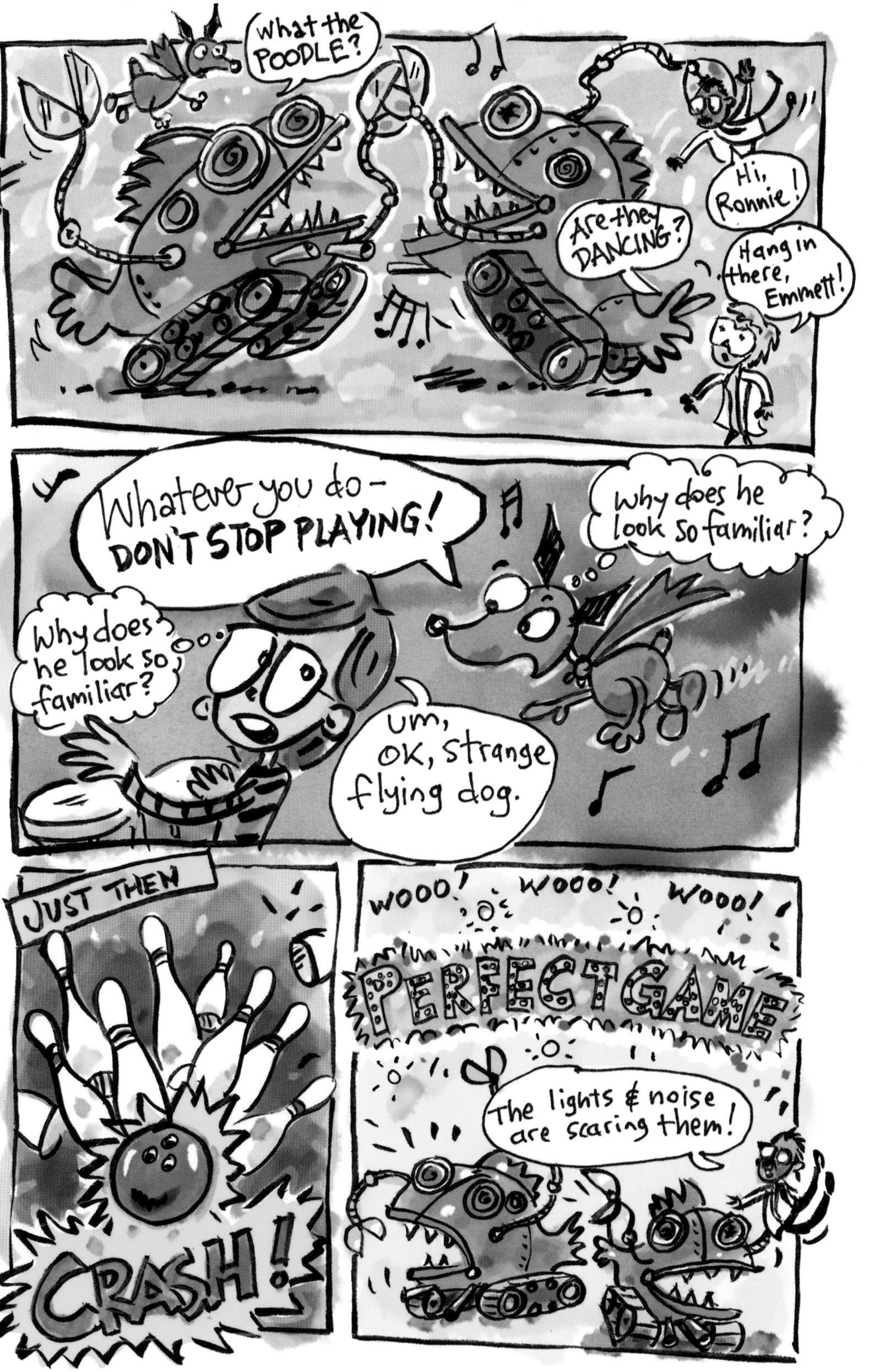
What the POODLE?
Hi, Ronnie!
Are they DANCING?
Hang in there, Emmett!
Whatever you do- DON'T STOP PLAYING!
Why does he look so familiar?
Why does he look so familiar?
Um, OK, strange flying dog.
JUST THEN
CRASH!
WOOO! WOOO! WOOO!
PERFECT GAME
The lights & noise are scaring them!

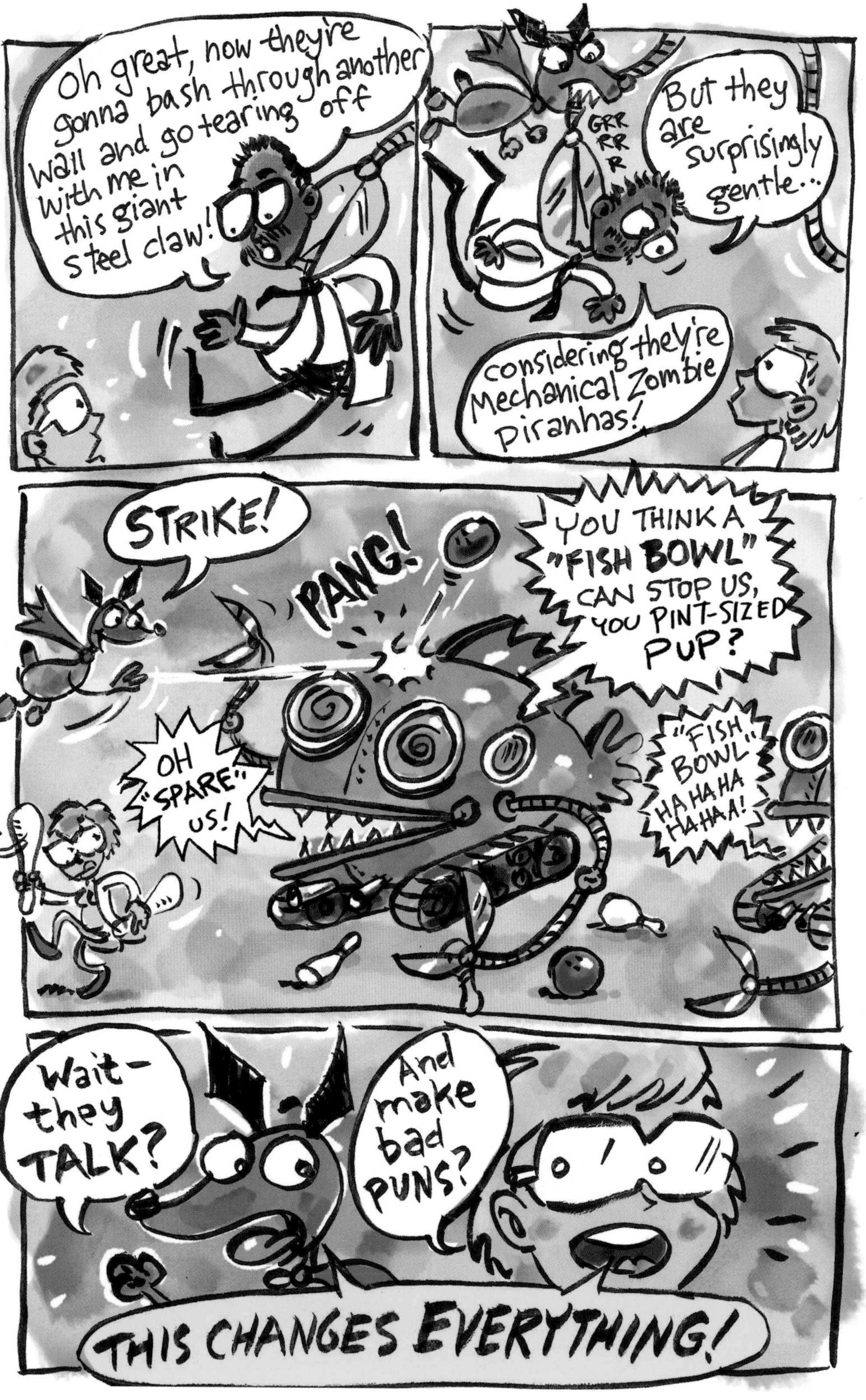
Oh great, now they're gonna bash through another wall and go tearing off with me in this giant steel claw!
GRR RR R
But they are surprisingly gentle...
considering they're Mechanical Zombie Piranhas!
STRIKE!
PANG!
YOU THINK A "FISH BOWL" CAN STOP US, YOU PINT-SIZED PUP?
OH "SPARE" US!
"FISH BOWL" HA HA HA HA HA A!
Wait- they TALK?
And make bad PUNS?
THIS CHANGES EVERYTHING!

CHAPTER 7: PAPER OR PLASTIC?

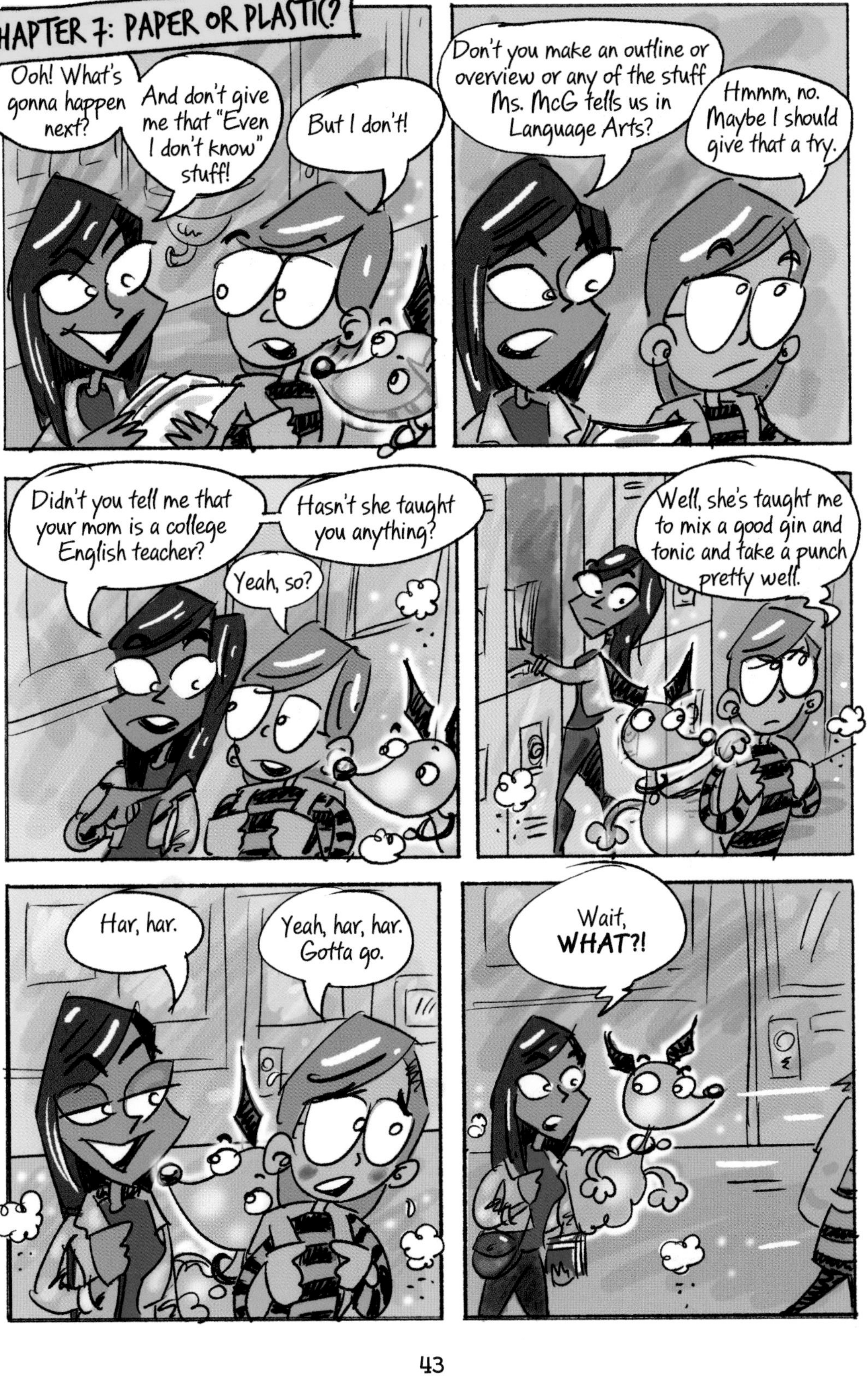
Ooh! What's gonna happen next?
And don't give me that "Even I don't know" stuff!
But I don't!
Don't you make an outline or overview or any of the stuff Ms. McG tells us in Language Arts?
Hmmm, no. Maybe I should give that a try.
Didn't you tell me that your mom is a college English teacher?
Hasn't she taught you anything?
Yeah, so?
Well, she's taught me to mix a good gin and tonic and take a punch pretty well.
Har, har.
Yeah, har, har. Gotta go.
Wait, WHAT?!

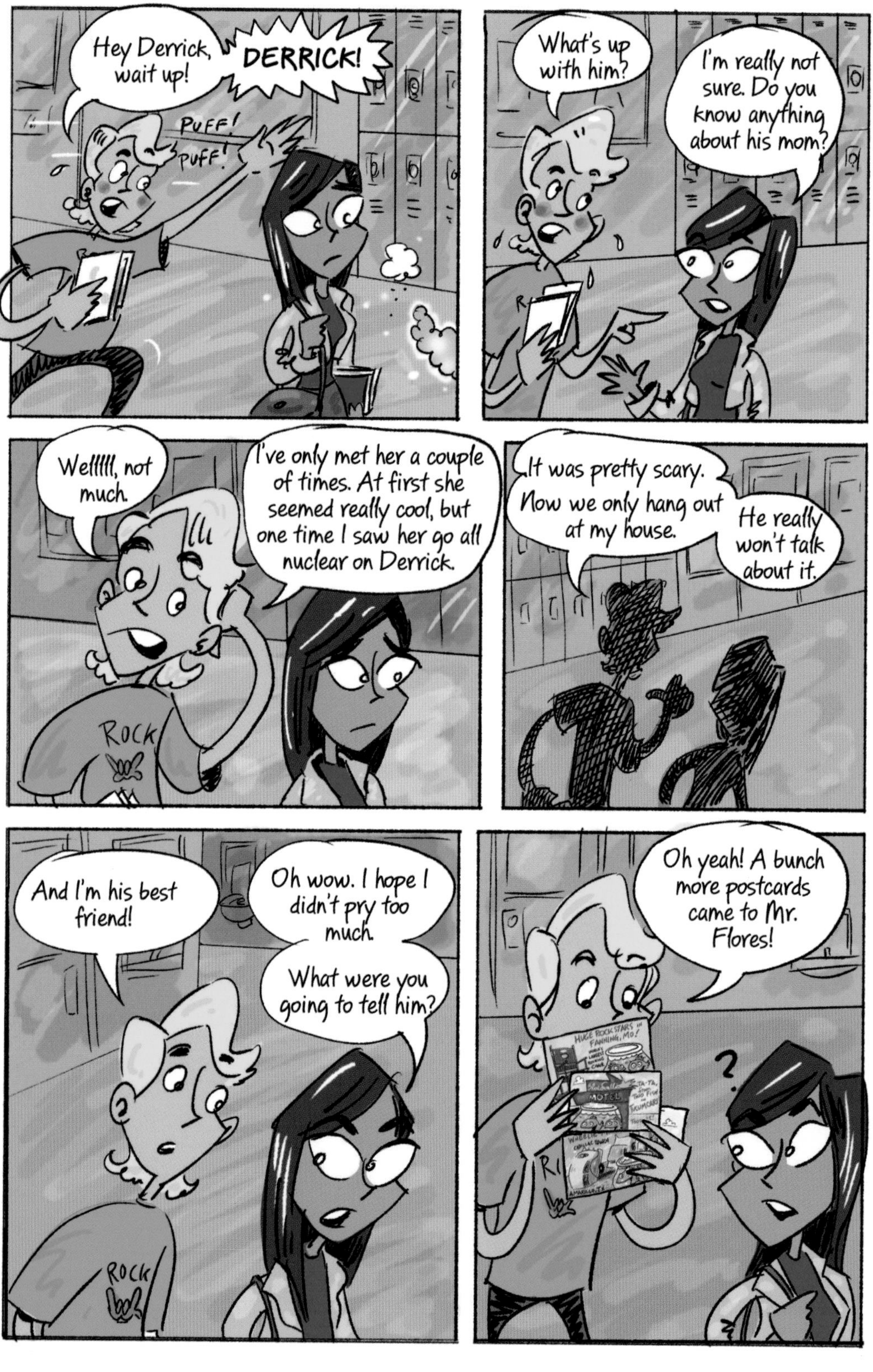
Hey Derrick, wait up!
DERRICK!
PUFF! PUFF!
What's up with him?
I'm really not sure. Do you know anything about his mom?
Welllll, not much.
I've only met her a couple of times. At first she seemed really cool, but one time I saw her go all nuclear on Derrick.
It was pretty scary. Now we only hang out at my house.
He really won't talk about it.
And I'm his best friend!
Oh wow. I hope I didn't pry too much.
What were you going to tell him?
Oh yeah! A bunch more postcards came to Mr. Flores!
?
HUGE ROCK STARS IN FANNING, MO!
MOTEL
WHEELS CADILLAC RANCH AMARILLO
ROCK

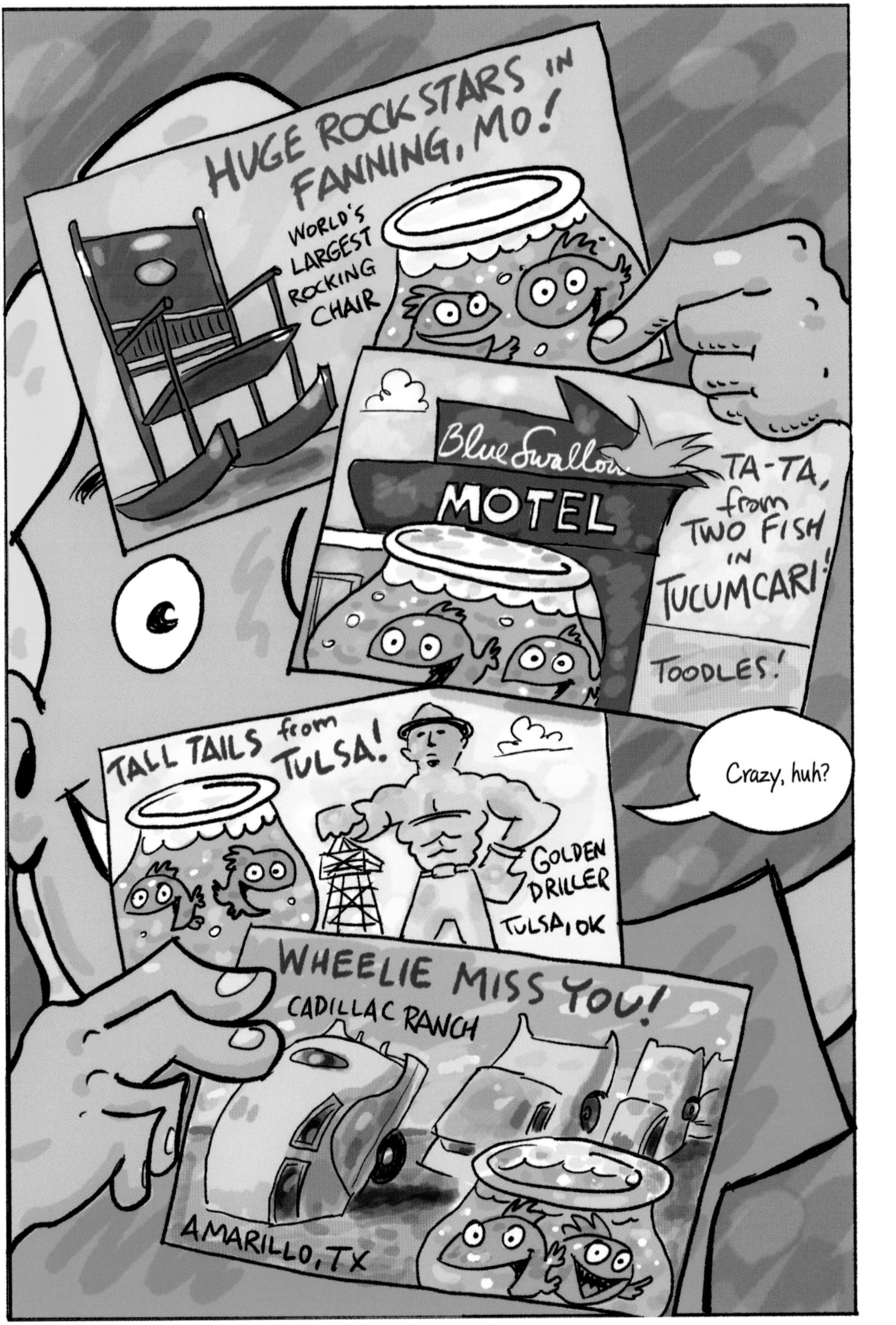
HUGE ROCK STARS IN FANNING, MO!
WORLD'S LARGEST ROCKING CHAIR
Blue Swallow
MOTEL
TA-TA, from TWO FISH IN TUCUMCARI!
TOODLES!
TALL TAILS from TULSA!
GOLDEN DRILLER
TULSA, OK
Crazy, huh?
WHEELIE MISS YOU!
CADILLAC RANCH
AMARILLO, TX

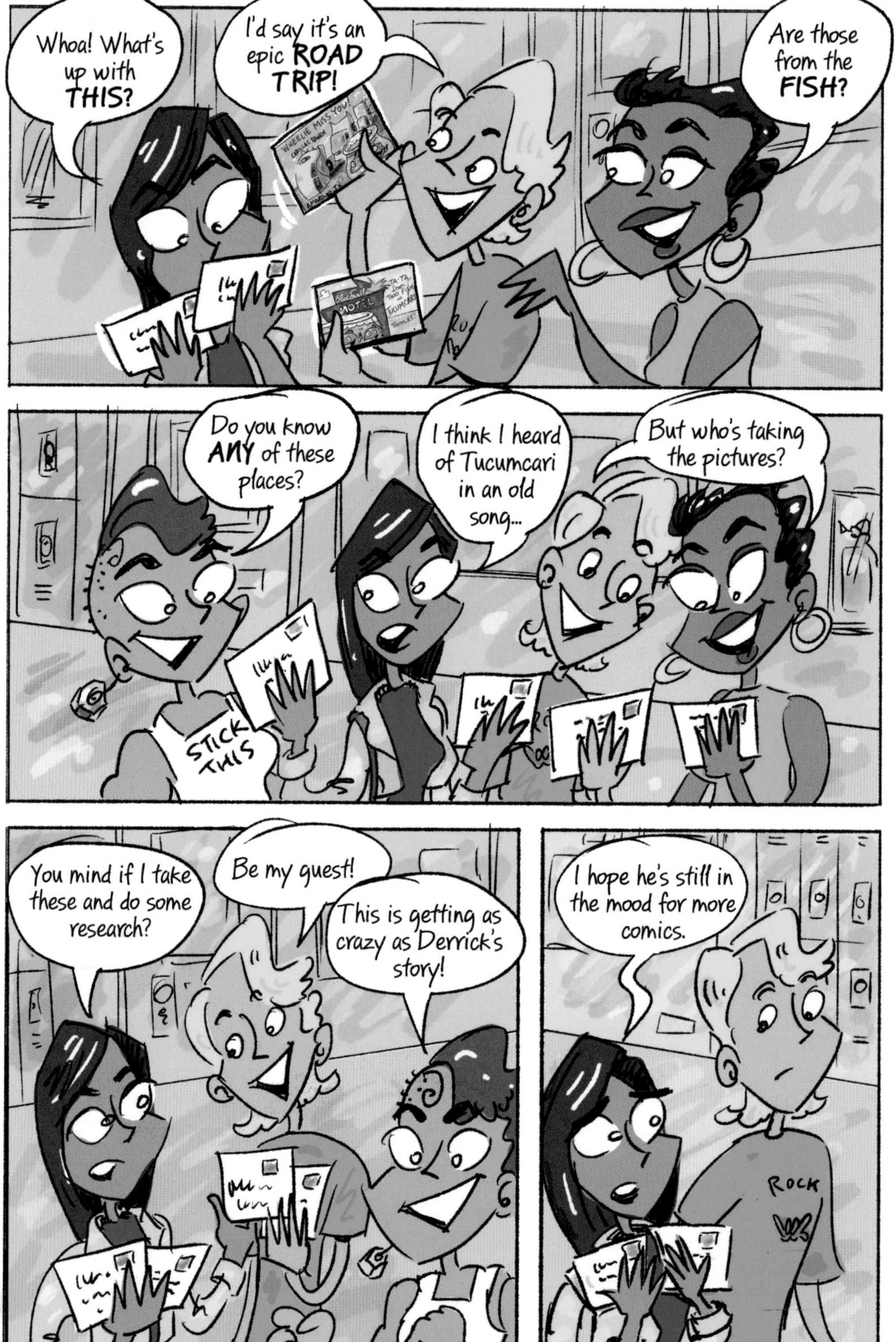

Whoa! What's up with THIS?
I'd say it's an epic ROAD TRIP!
Are those from the FISH?
Do you know ANY of these places?
I think I heard of Tucumcari in an old song...
But who's taking the pictures?
STICK THIS
You mind if I take these and do some research?
Be my guest!
This is getting as crazy as Derrick's story!
I hope he's still in the mood for more comics.
ROCK

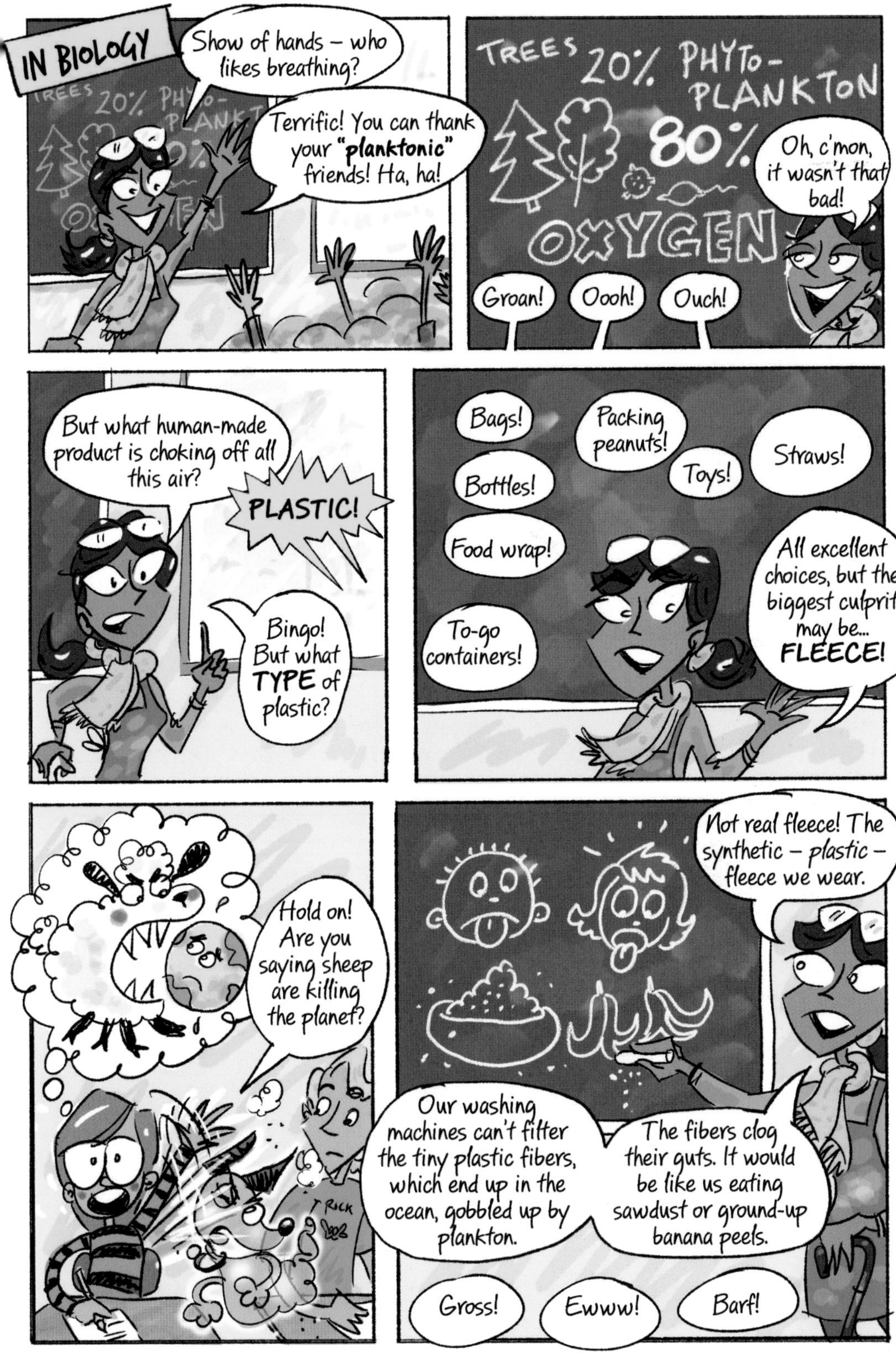
IN BIOLOGY
Show of hands – who likes breathing?
Terrific! You can thank your "planktonic" friends! Ha, ha!
TREES 20% PHYTO-PLANKTON 80% OXYGEN
Oh, c'mon, it wasn't that bad!
Groan!
Oooh!
Ouch!
But what human-made product is choking off all this air?
PLASTIC!
Bingo! But what TYPE of plastic?
Bags!
Packing peanuts!
Straws!
Toys!
Bottles!
Food wrap!
To-go containers!
All excellent choices, but the biggest culprit may be... FLEECE!
Hold on! Are you saying sheep are killing the planet?
Not real fleece! The synthetic – plastic – fleece we wear.
Our washing machines can't filter the tiny plastic fibers, which end up in the ocean, gobbled up by plankton.
The fibers clog their guts. It would be like us eating sawdust or ground-up banana peels.
Gross!
Ewww!
Barf!

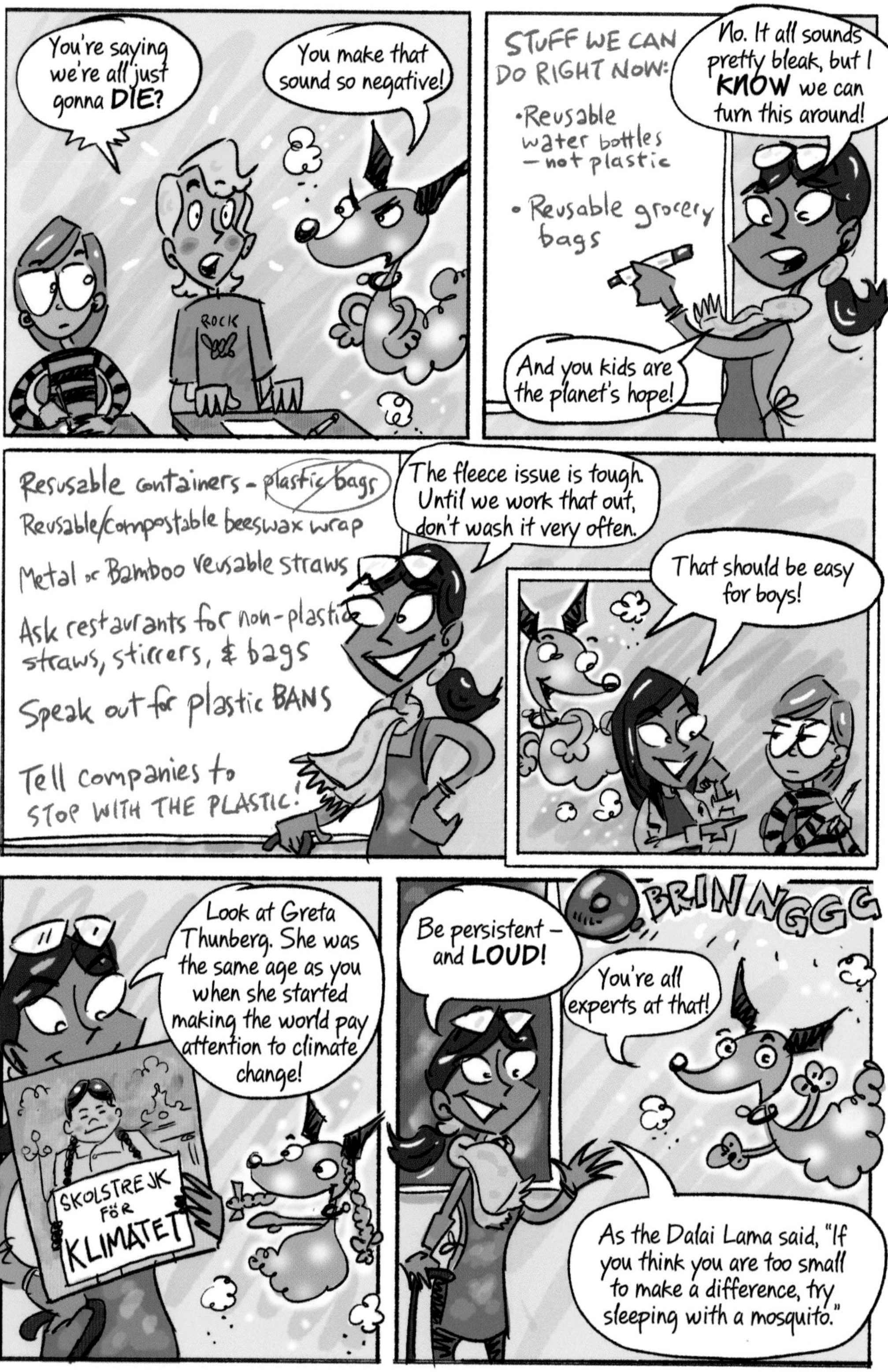

You're saying we're all just gonna **DIE**?
You make that sound so negative!
STUFF WE CAN DO RIGHT NOW:
•Reusable water bottles —not plastic
•Reusable grocery bags
No. It all sounds pretty bleak, but I **KNOW** we can turn this around!
And you kids are the planet's hope!
Resusable containers - ~~plastic bags~~
Reusable/compostable beeswax wrap
Metal or Bamboo reusable straws
Ask restaurants for non-plastic straws, stirrers, & bags
Speak out for plastic BANS
Tell companies to STOP WITH THE PLASTIC!
The fleece issue is tough. Until we work that out, don't wash it very often.
That should be easy for boys!
Look at Greta Thunberg. She was the same age as you when she started making the world pay attention to climate change!
SKOLSTREJK FÖR KLIMATET
Be persistent – and **LOUD**!
BRINNGGG
You're all experts at that!
As the Dalai Lama said, "If you think you are too small to make a difference, try sleeping with a mosquito."

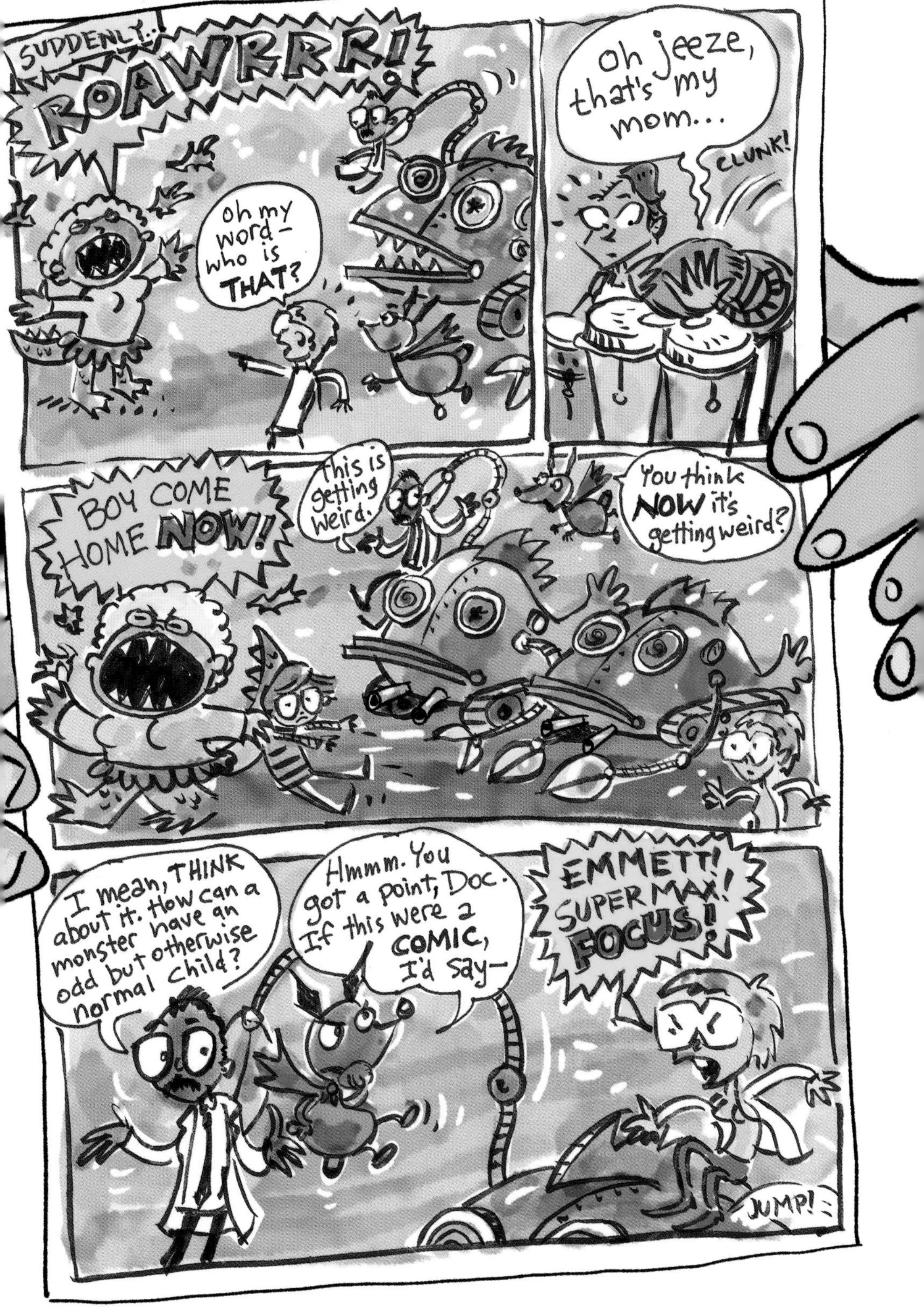
SUDDENLY...
ROAWRRR!
Oh my word— who is THAT?
Oh jeeze, that's my mom...
CLUNK!
BOY COME HOME NOW!
This is getting weird.
You think NOW it's getting weird?
I mean, THINK about it. How can a monster have an odd but otherwise normal child?
Hmmm. You got a point, Doc. If this were a COMIC, I'd say—
EMMETT! SUPER MAX! FOCUS!
JUMP!

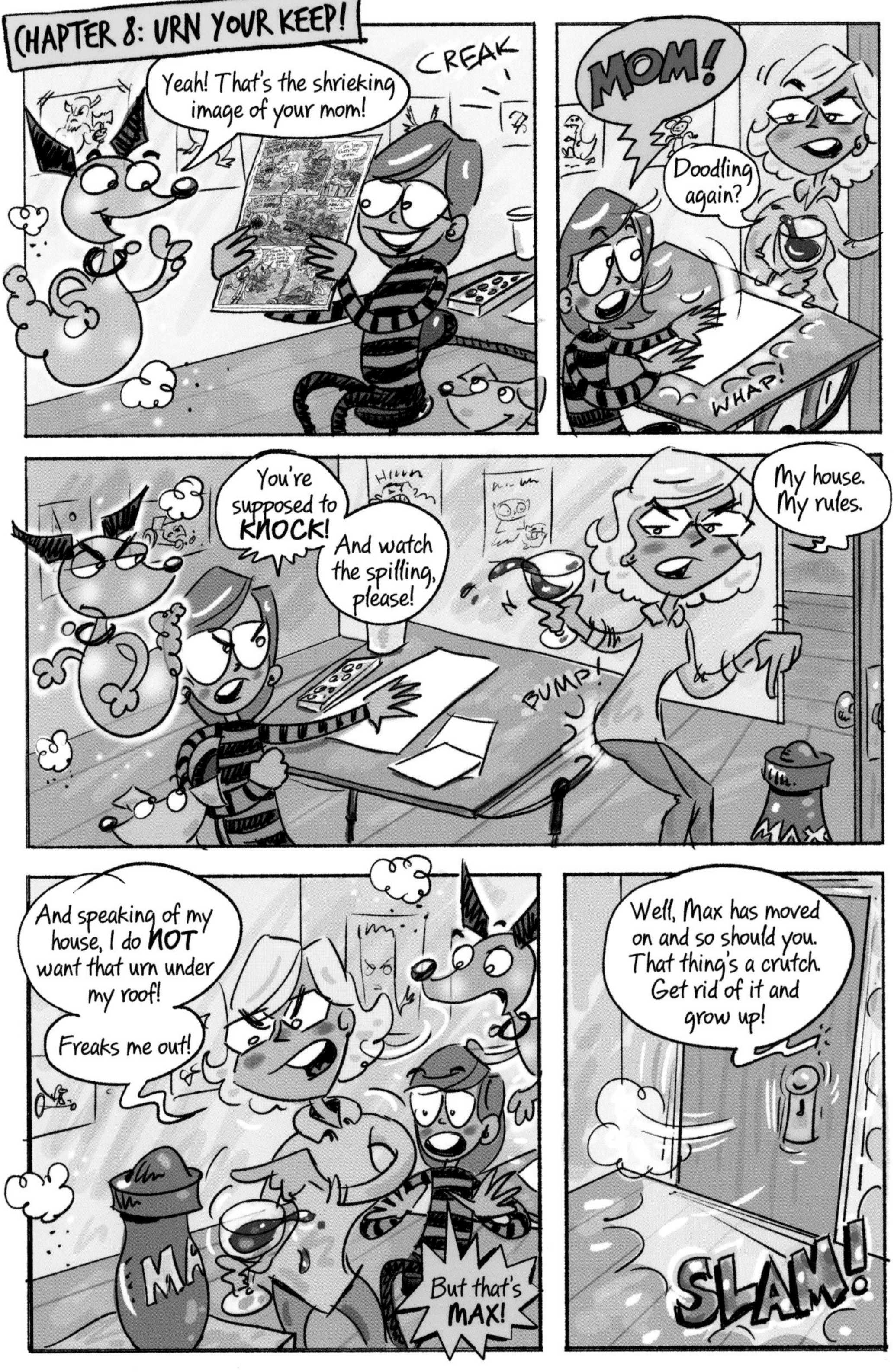

CHAPTER 8: URN YOUR KEEP!
Yeah! That's the shrieking image of your mom!
CREAK
MOM!
Doodling again?
WHAP!
You're supposed to KNOCK!
And watch the spilling, please!
My house. My rules.
BUMP!
And speaking of my house, I do NOT want that urn under my roof!
Freaks me out!
But that's MAX!
Well, Max has moved on and so should you. That thing's a crutch. Get rid of it and grow up!
SLAM!

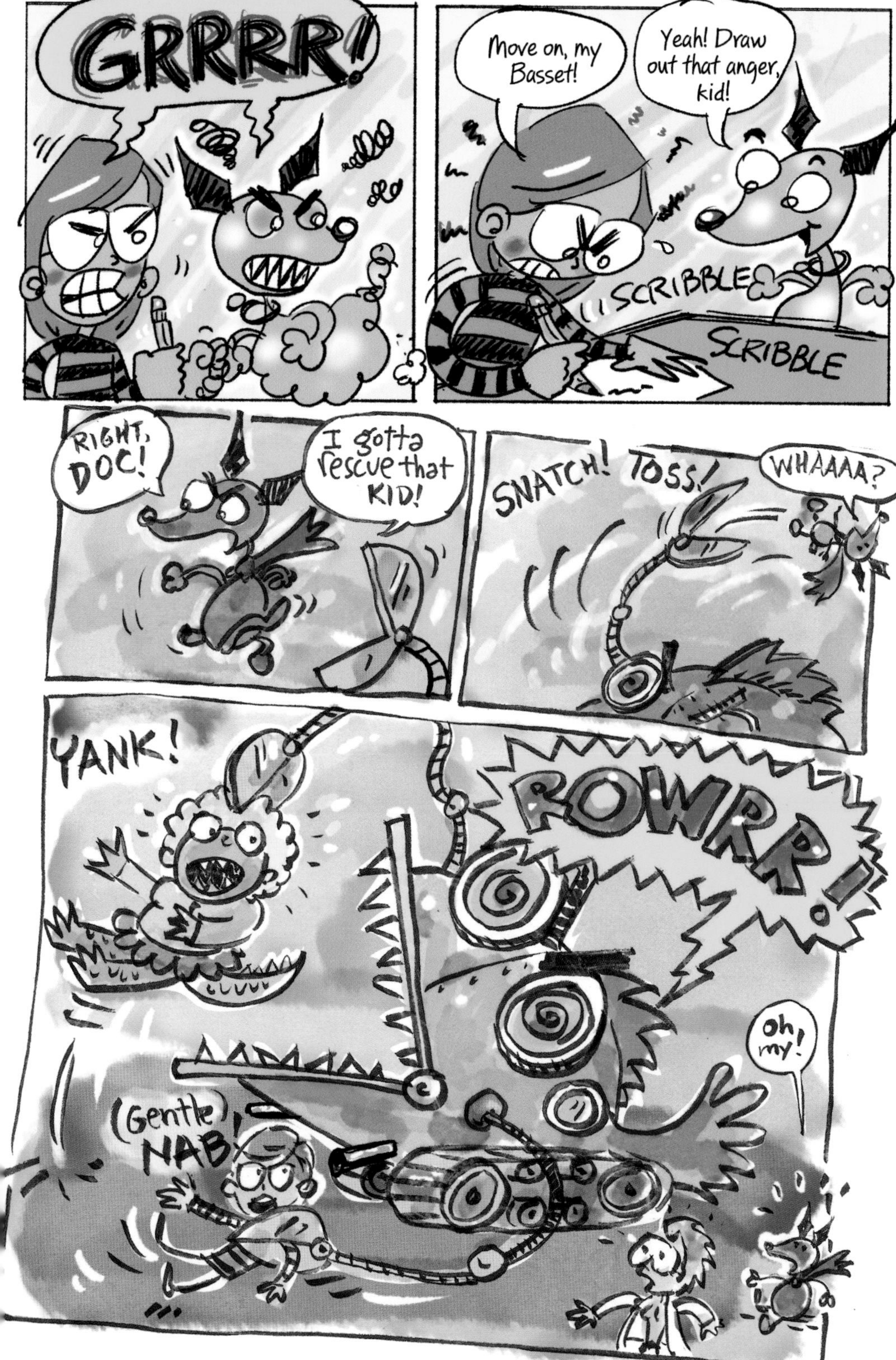
GRRRR!
Move on, my Basset!
Yeah! Draw out that anger, kid!
SCRIBBLE
SCRIBBLE
RIGHT, DOC!
I gotta rescue that KID!
SNATCH! TOSS!
WHAAAA?
YANK!
ROWRR!
Oh my!
(Gentle) NAB!

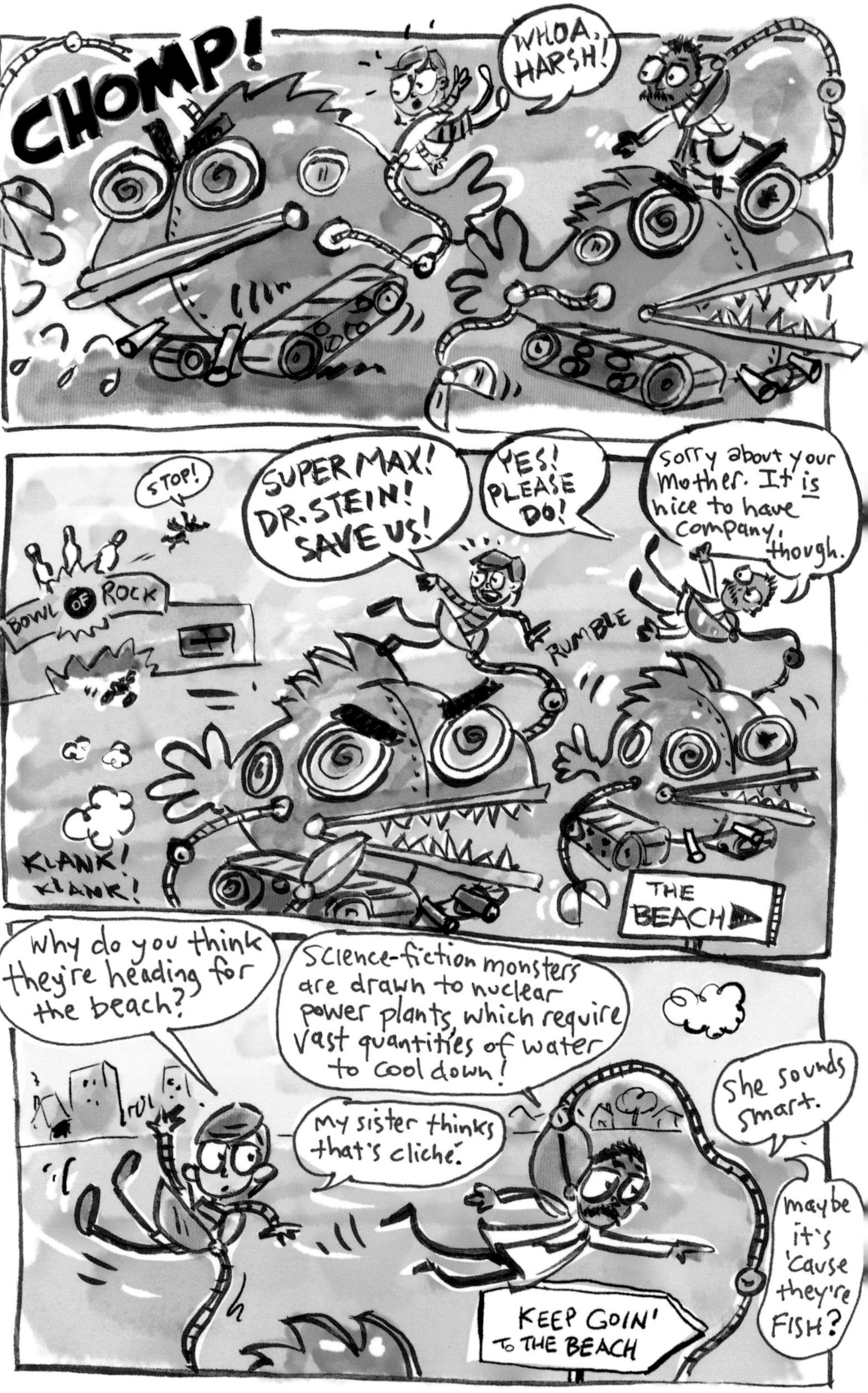
CHOMP!
WHOA, HARSH!
STOP!
BOWL OF ROCK
SUPER MAX! DR. STEIN! SAVE US!
YES! PLEASE DO!
Sorry about your mother. It is nice to have company, though.
RUMBLE
KLANK! KLANK!
THE BEACH
Why do you think they're heading for the beach?
Science-fiction monsters are drawn to nuclear power plants, which require vast quantities of water to cool down!
My sister thinks that's cliché.
She sounds smart.
maybe it's 'cause they're FISH?
KEEP GOIN' TO THE BEACH

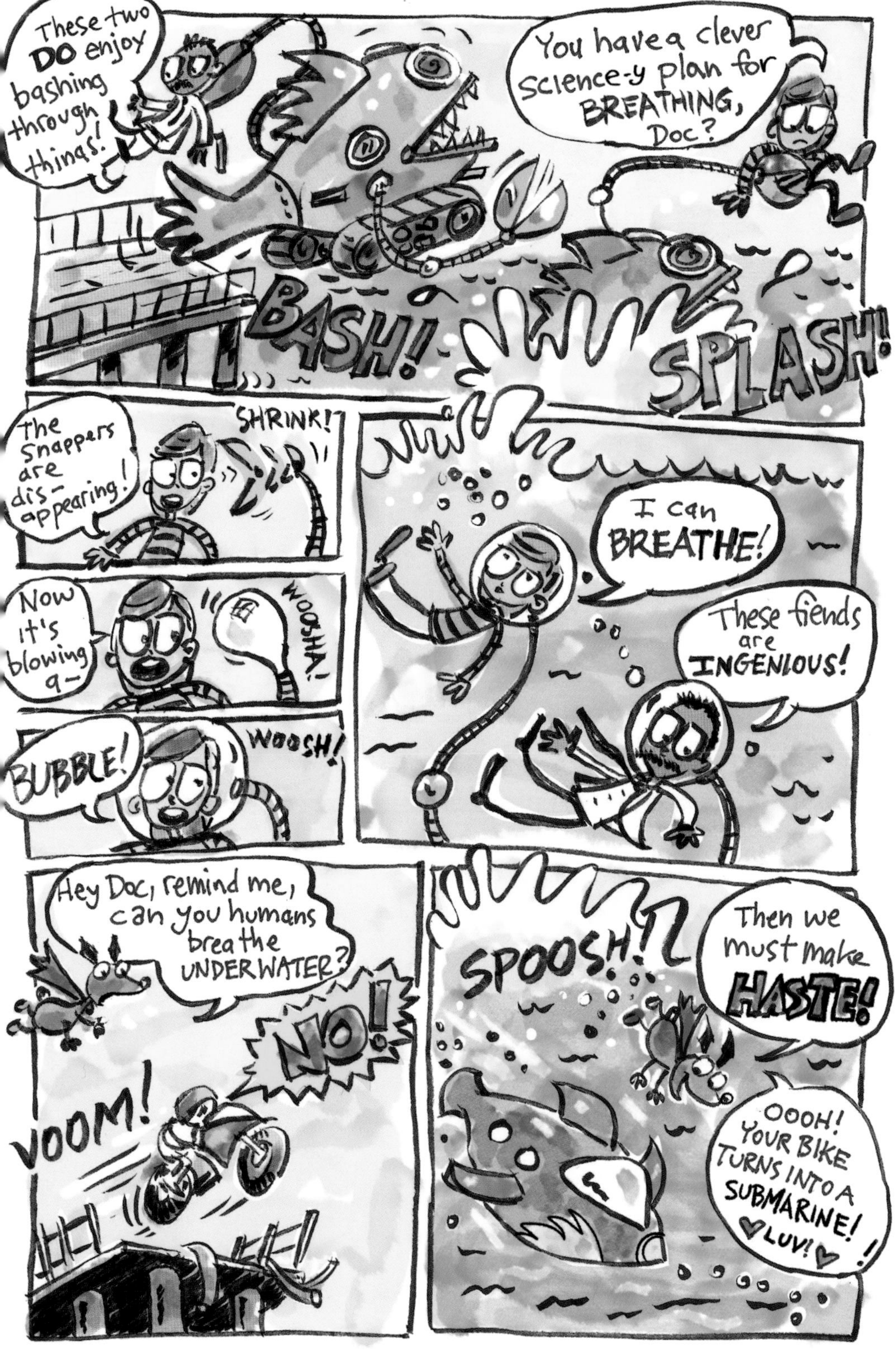

These two DO enjoy bashing through things!
You have a clever Science-y plan for BREATHING, Doc?
BASH!
SPLASH!
The snappers are dis-appearing!
SHRINK!
Now it's blowing a—
WOOSHA!
BUBBLE!
WOOSH!
I can BREATHE!
These fiends are INGENIOUS!
Hey Doc, remind me, can you humans breathe UNDERWATER?
NO!
VOOM!
SPOOSH!
Then we must make HASTE!
OOOH! YOUR BIKE TURNS INTO A SUBMARINE! LUV!

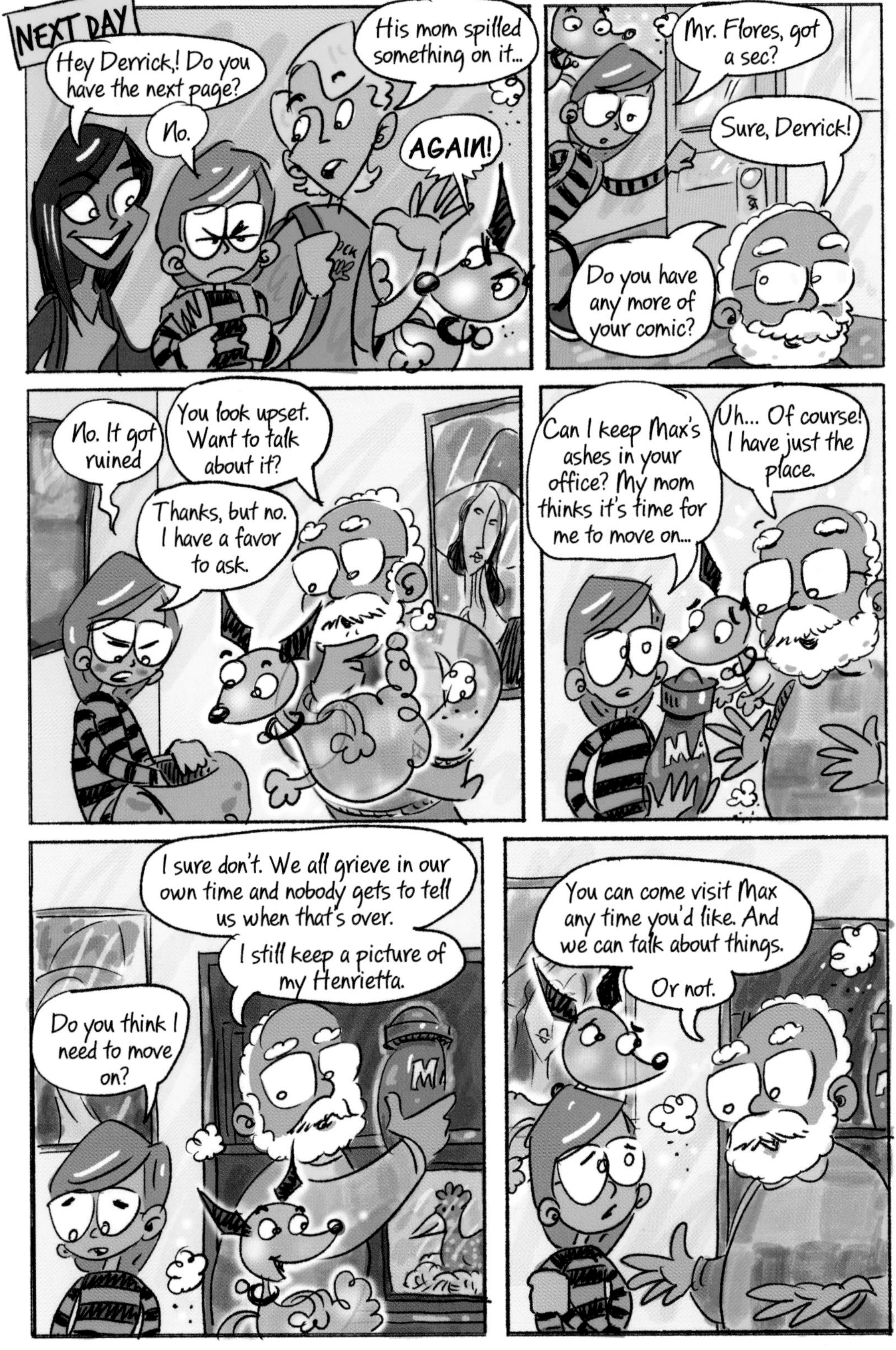
NEXT DAY
Hey Derrick! Do you have the next page?
No.
His mom spilled something on it...
AGAIN!
Mr. Flores, got a sec?
Sure, Derrick!
Do you have any more of your comic?
No. It got ruined
You look upset. Want to talk about it?
Thanks, but no. I have a favor to ask.
Can I keep Max's ashes in your office? My mom thinks it's time for me to move on...
Uh... Of course! I have just the place.
Do you think I need to move on?
I sure don't. We all grieve in our own time and nobody gets to tell us when that's over.
I still keep a picture of my Henrietta.
You can come visit Max any time you'd like. And we can talk about things.
Or not.

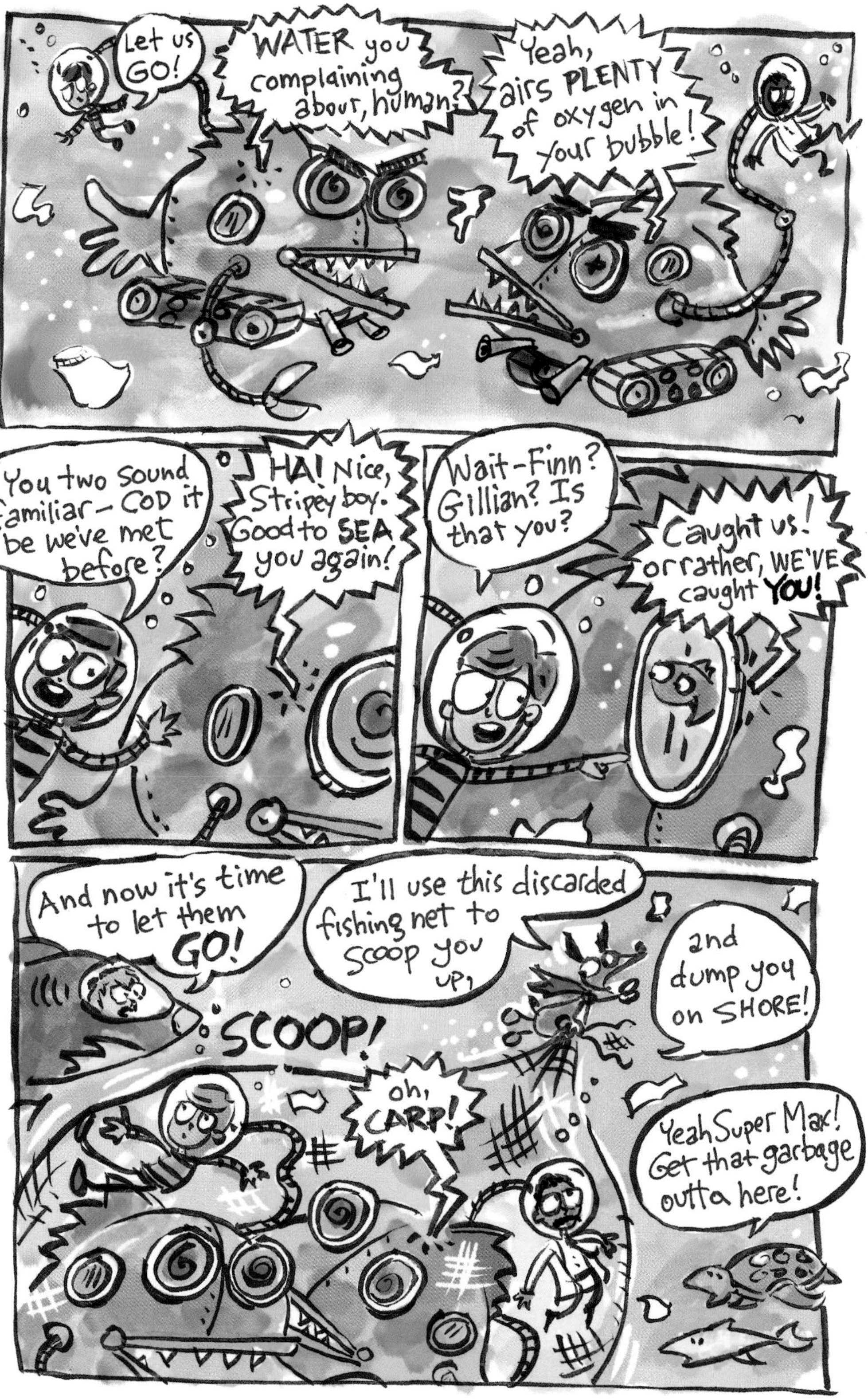
Let us GO!
WATER you complaining about, human?
Yeah, airs PLENTY of oxygen in your bubble!
You two sound familiar— COD it be we've met before?
HA! Nice, Stripey boy. Good to SEA you again!
Wait-Finn? Gillian? Is that you?
Caught us! orrather, WE'VE caught YOU!
And now it's time to let them GO!
I'll use this discarded fishing net to scoop you up,
and dump you on SHORE!
SCOOP!
oh, CARP!
Yeah Super Max! Get that garbage outta here!

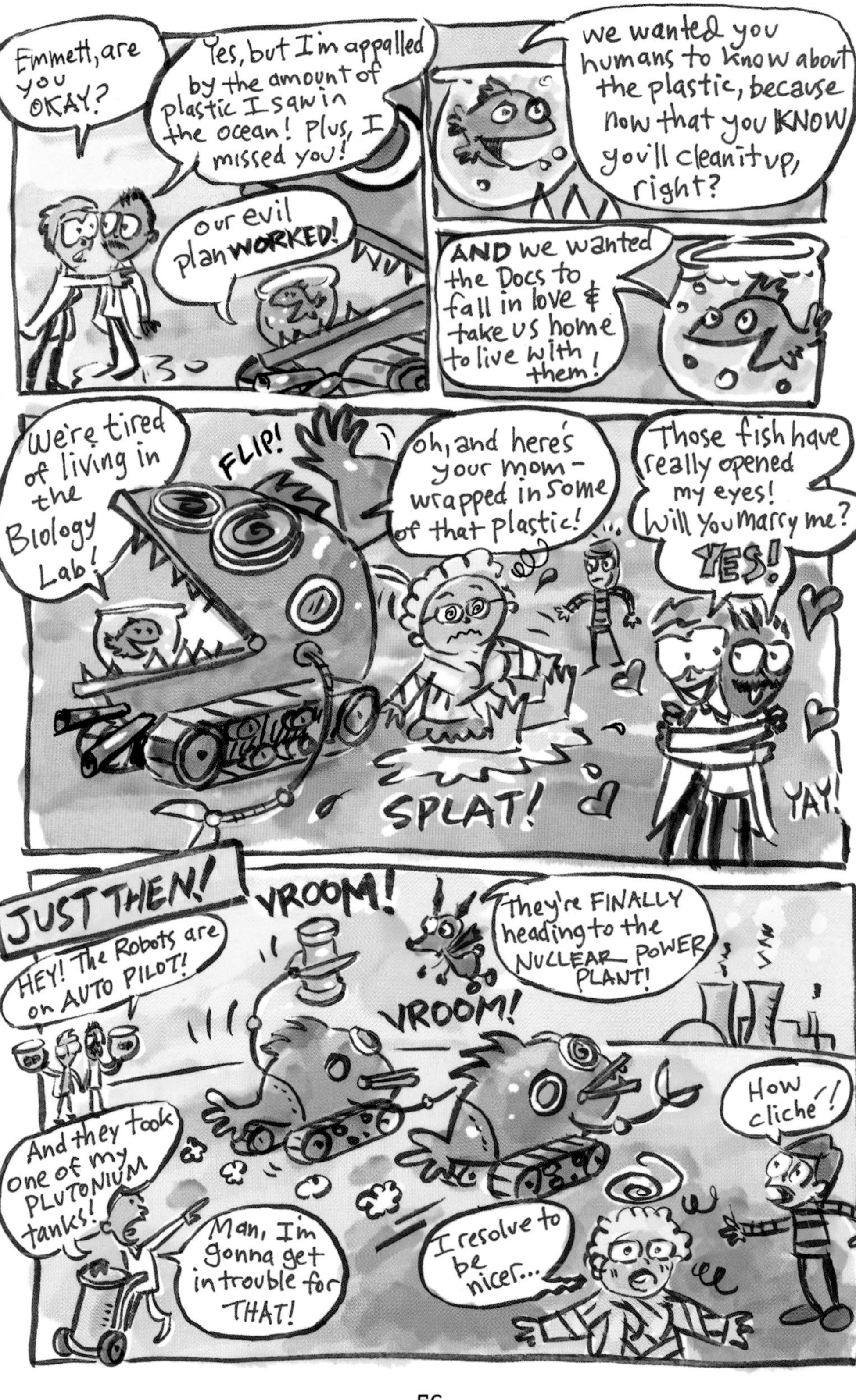
Emmett, are you OKAY?
Yes, but I'm appalled by the amount of plastic I saw in the ocean! Plus, I missed you!
our evil plan WORKED!
we wanted you humans to know about the plastic, because now that you KNOW you'll clean it up, right?
AND we wanted the Docs to fall in love & take us home to live with them!
We're tired of living in the Biology Lab!
FLIP!
Oh, and here's your mom - wrapped in some of that plastic!
Those fish have really opened my eyes! Will you marry me?
YES!
SPLAT!
YAY!
JUST THEN!
VROOM!
HEY! The Robots are on AUTO PILOT!
They're FINALLY heading to the NUCLEAR POWER PLANT!
VROOM!
How cliché!
And they took one of my PLUTONIUM tanks!
Man, I'm gonna get in trouble for THAT!
I resolve to be nicer...

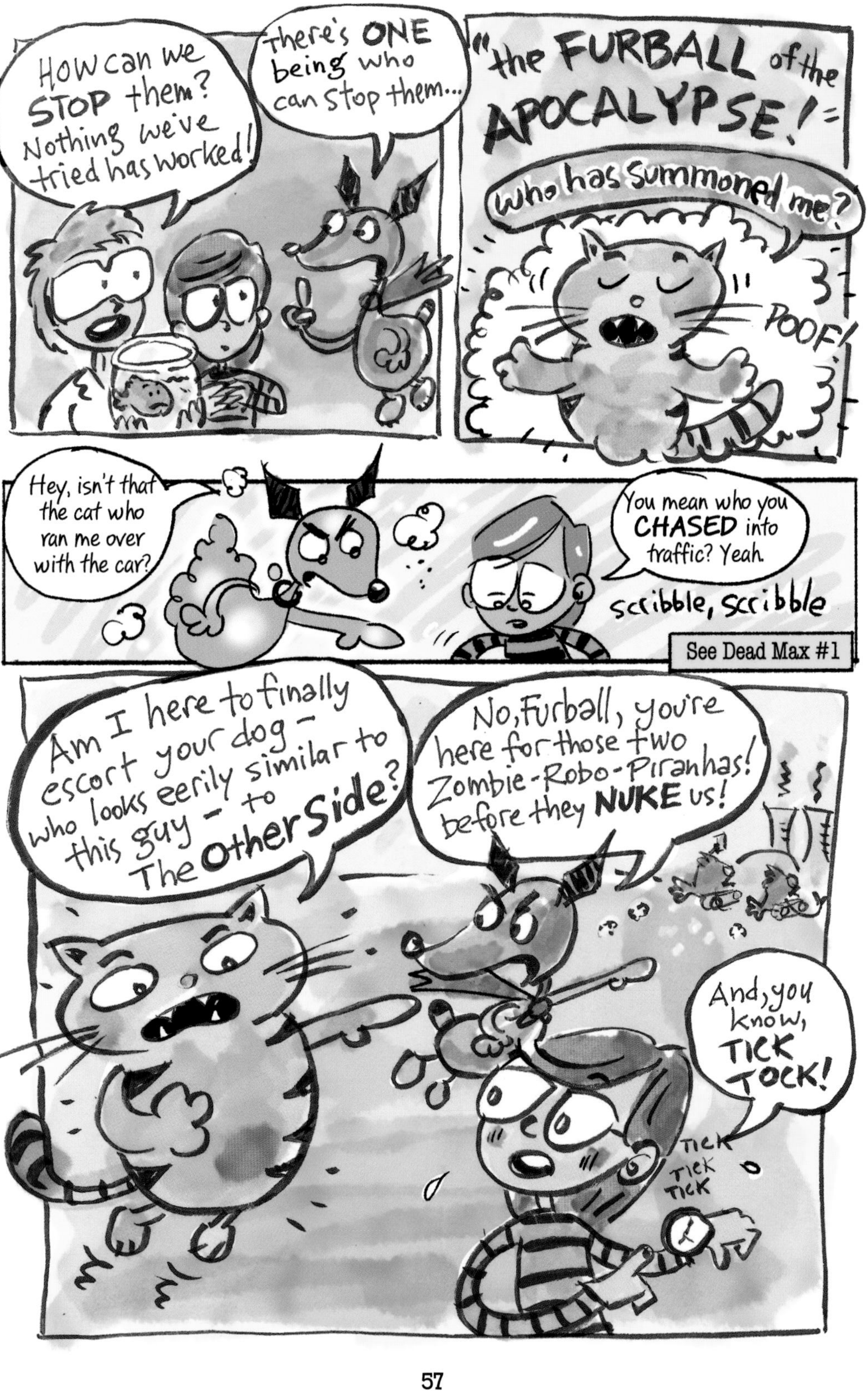
How can we STOP them? Nothing we've tried has worked!
There's ONE being who can stop them...
"the FURBALL of the APOCALYPSE!"
who has summoned me?
POOF!
Hey, isn't that the cat who ran me over with the car?
You mean who you CHASED into traffic? Yeah.
scribble, scribble
See Dead Max #1
Am I here to finally escort your dog - who looks eerily similar to this guy - to The Other Side?
No, Furball, you're here for those two Zombie-Robo-Piranhas! before they NUKE us!
And, you know, TICK TOCK!
TICK
TICK
TICK

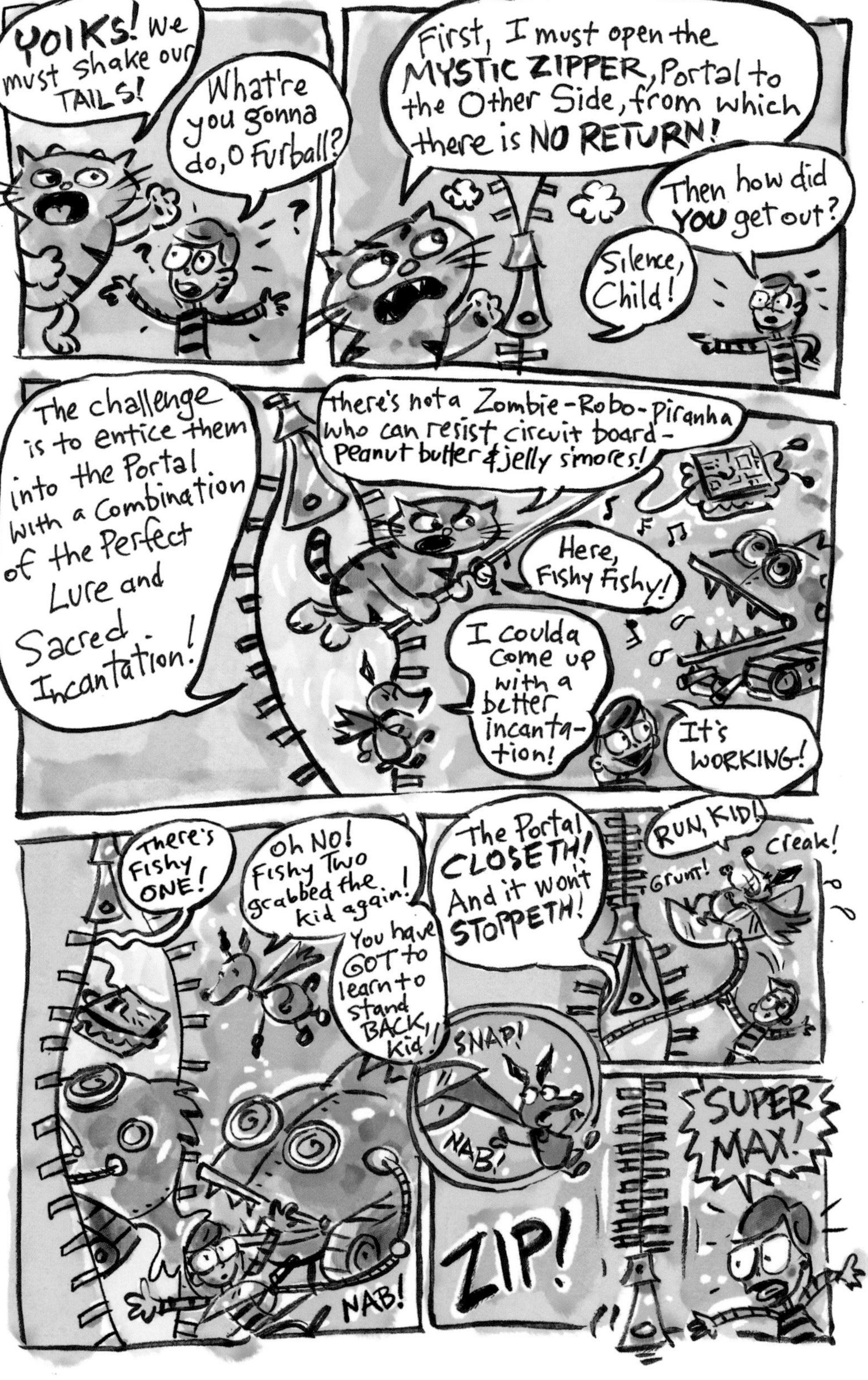

YOIKS! We must shake our TAILS!
What're you gonna do, O Furball?
First, I must open the MYSTIC ZIPPER, Portal to the Other Side, from which there is NO RETURN!
Then how did YOU get out?
Silence, Child!
The challenge is to entice them into the Portal with a Combination of the Perfect Lure and Sacred Incantation!
There's not a Zombie-Robo-Piranha who can resist circuit board-Peanut butter & jelly s'mores!
Here, Fishy Fishy!
I coulda come up with a better incantation!
It's WORKING!
There's Fishy ONE!
Oh NO! Fishy Two grabbed the kid again!
You have GOT to learn to stand BACK, Kid!
NAB!
SNAP!
NAB!
The Portal CLOSETH! And it won't STOPPETH!
RUN, KID!
GRUNT!
Creak!
ZIP!
SUPER MAX!

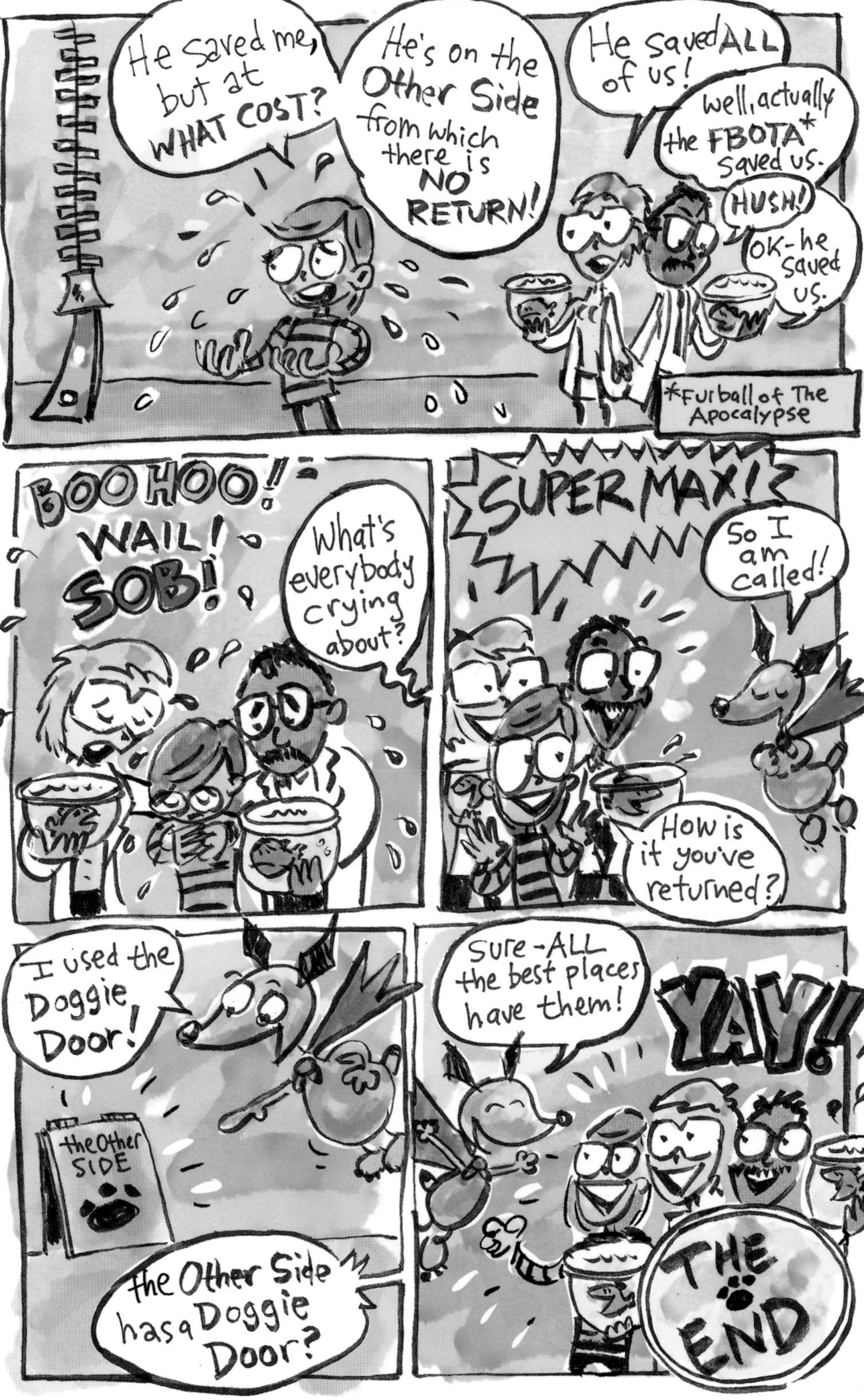
He saved me, but at WHAT COST?
He's on the Other Side from which there is NO RETURN!
He saved ALL of us!
well, actually the FBOTA* saved us.
HUSH!
OK-he saved us.
*Furball of The Apocalypse
BOO HOO!
WAIL!
SOB!
What's everybody crying about?
SUPER MAX!
So I am called!
How is it you've returned?
I used the Doggie Door!
the Other SIDE
the Other Side has a Doggie Door?
Sure-ALL the best places have them!
YAY!
THE END

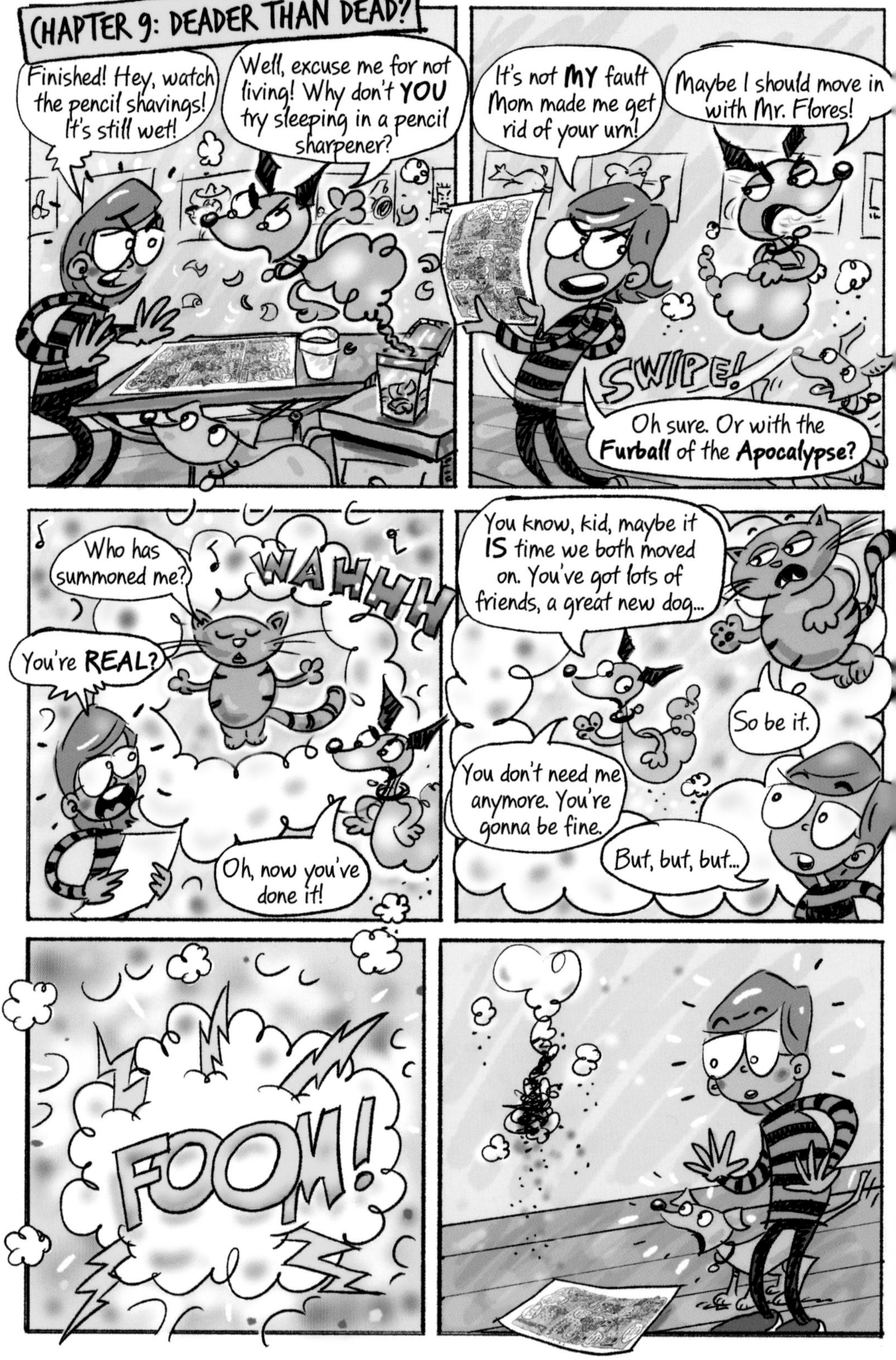

CHAPTER 9: DEADER THAN DEAD?
Finished! Hey, watch the pencil shavings! It's still wet!
Well, excuse me for not living! Why don't YOU try sleeping in a pencil sharpener?
It's not MY fault Mom made me get rid of your urn!
Maybe I should move in with Mr. Flores!
SWIPE!
Oh sure. Or with the Furball of the Apocalypse?
Who has summoned me?
WAHHHH
You're REAL?
Oh, now you've done it!
You know, kid, maybe it IS time we both moved on. You've got lots of friends, a great new dog...
You don't need me anymore. You're gonna be fine.
So be it.
But, but, but...
FOOM!

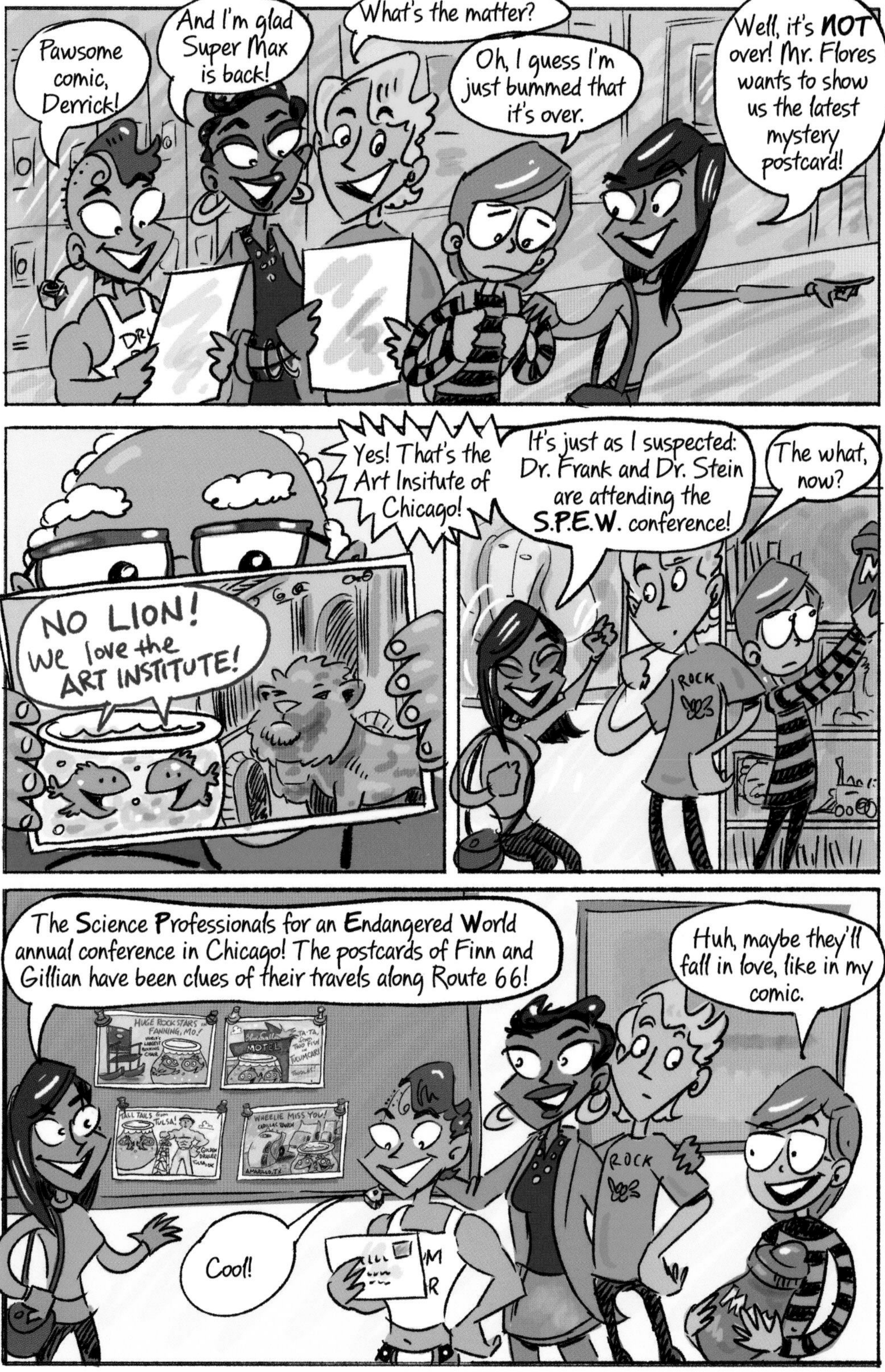
Pawsome comic, Derrick!
And I'm glad Super Max is back!
What's the matter?
Oh, I guess I'm just bummed that it's over.
Well, it's NOT over! Mr. Flores wants to show us the latest mystery postcard!
NO LION! We love the ART INSTITUTE!
Yes! That's the Art Insitute of Chicago!
It's just as I suspected: Dr. Frank and Dr. Stein are attending the S.P.E.W. conference!
The what, now?
ROCK
The Science Professionals for an Endangered World annual conference in Chicago! The postcards of Finn and Gillian have been clues of their travels along Route 66!
Huh, maybe they'll fall in love, like in my comic.
HUGE ROCKSTARS in FANNING, MO!
MOTEL
TALL TAILS from TULSA!
WHEELIE MISS YOU!
ROCK
Cool!

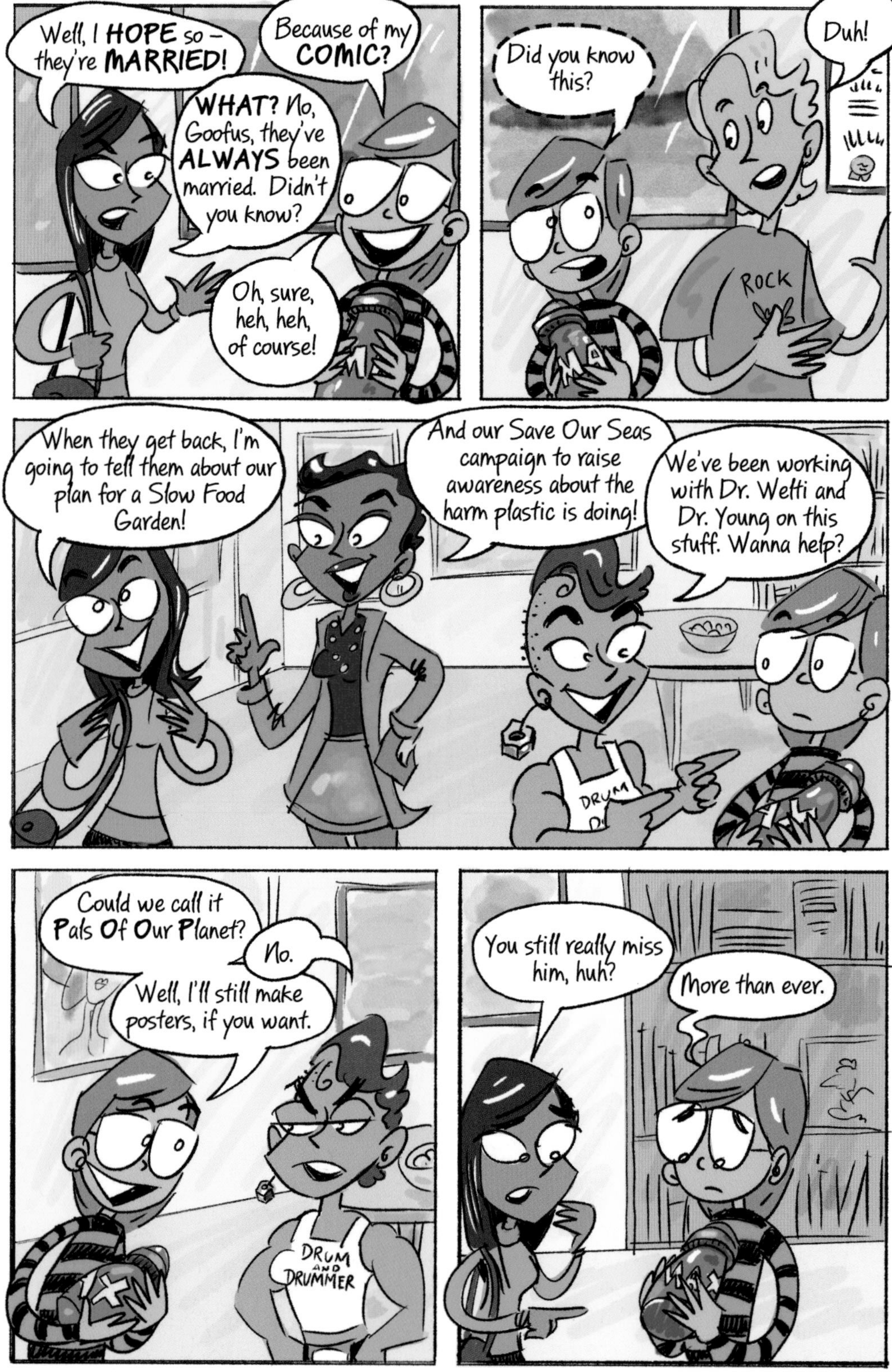
Well, I HOPE so – they're MARRIED!
Because of my COMIC?
WHAT? No, Goofus, they've ALWAYS been married. Didn't you know?
Oh, sure, heh, heh, of course!
Did you know this?
Duh!
ROCK
When they get back, I'm going to tell them about our plan for a Slow Food Garden!
And our Save Our Seas campaign to raise awareness about the harm plastic is doing!
We've been working with Dr. Welti and Dr. Young on this stuff. Wanna help?
Could we call it Pals Of Our Planet?
No.
Well, I'll still make posters, if you want.
DRUM AND DRUMMER
You still really miss him, huh?
More than ever.

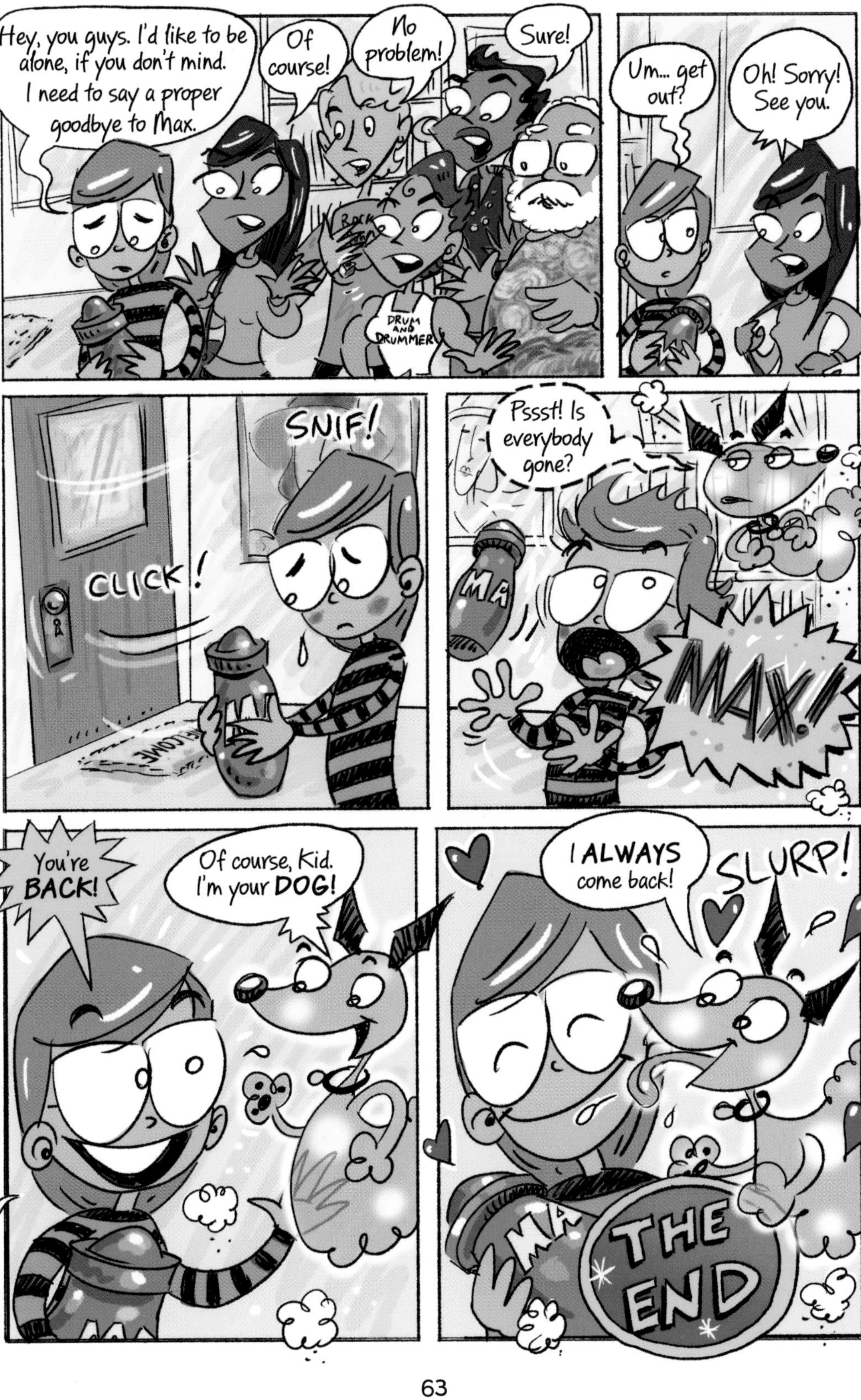

Hey, you guys. I'd like to be alone, if you don't mind. I need to say a proper goodbye to Max.
Of course!
No problem!
Sure!
ROCK
DRUM AND DRUMMER
Um... get out?
Oh! Sorry! See you.
SNIF!
CLICK!
WELCOME
Pssst! Is everybody gone?
MAX!
You're BACK!
Of course, Kid. I'm your DOG!
I ALWAYS come back!
SLURP!
THE END

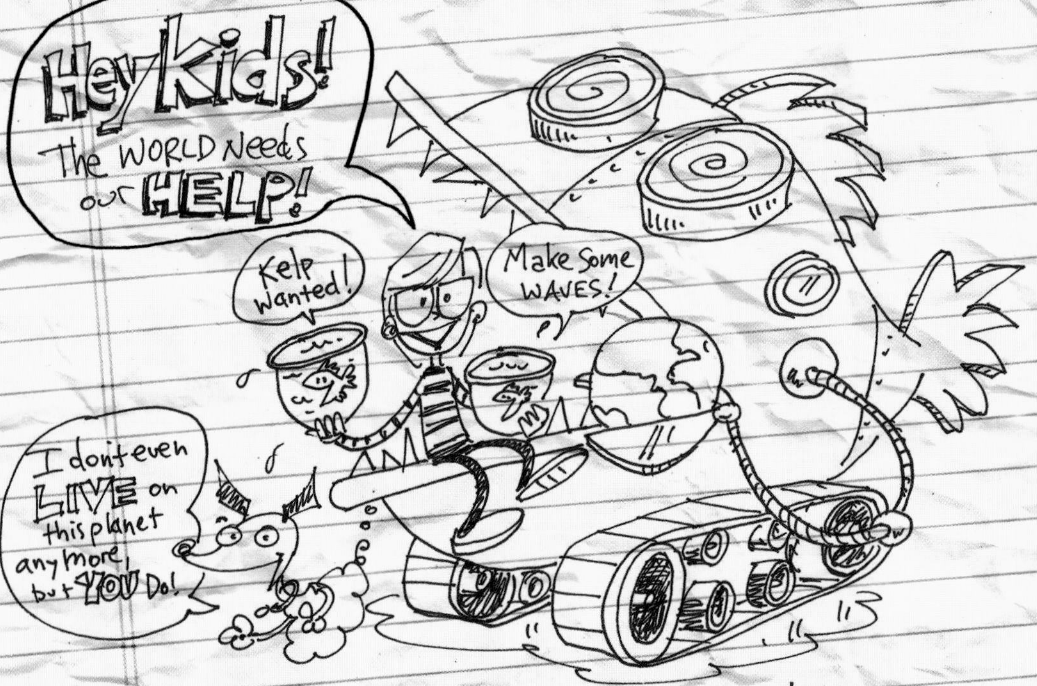
Hey Kids! The WORLD Needs our HELP!
Kelp wanted!
Make Some WAVES!
I don't even LIVE on this planet anymore, but YOU Do!

But what can a KID do? PLENTY!

Besides the stuff on p.48, here are a few websites for ideas:

www.planktonchronicles.org

www.storyofstuff.org

@GretaThunbergSweden

Dana lives and draws near the Salish Sea, on the Olympic Peninsula of Washington State with his sweet wife, Vicki, Bennie the barky dog and Max, the talky ex-dog. Dana's favorite color is dog and his favorite vegetable is peanut butter. Dana would love to see your comics and pictures of your pets! Or to visit your school! Contact info and other stuff at www.danajsullivan.com.

WE ALL NEED HELP SOMETIMES! (trust me on this) Your school counselor is a great person to start with. What could it hurt? They like kids and remember what it was like to be one.

Here's some online help too. For general, "What's going on with me?" stuff, these are two excellent CONFIDENTIAL resources:

Crisis Text Line: 741-741 (USA) or 686868 (Canada) to connect with an online volunteer

National Suicide Prevention Lifeline: 1-800-273-TALK (8255) suicidepreventionlifeline.org

And please get this into your noggin: **YOU ARE NOT ALONE!** Really.